W9-CCP-086

# MEMBERS OF THE FAMILY

*Helene Hardaway* has been married to Merrick for nearly fifty years. Her three daughters no longer speak to each other. She'll do *anything* to reunite her family.

*Merrick Hardaway* loves his wife more today than he did when he first married her. He knows how she misses their children, and he'll do *anything* to make her happy.

*Megan Hardaway* is the oldest of the Hardaway sisters. Every time she comes home to Hurricane Beach, she's reminded of the tragedy. So she stays away.

*Amy Hardaway*, middle daughter, always played the role of peacemaker when the girls were younger. Now, although she longs for the closeness she used to have with her sisters, she's about to do something that might sever all relationships for good.

*Jon Costas.* He'd married one Hardaway girl when they'd both been too young to know better. Now he's falling in love with his ex-sister-in-law, Amy. And his timing couldn't be worse.

*Lisa Hardaway* is the baby of the family. But her secret is so painful, she is unable—and unwilling—to share it with her sisters.

Dear Reader,

Growing up in Alabama meant lazy summer days spent on Florida's Gulf Coast beaches. The sun was blazing, the water gentle and the sand sugar-fine and just as white. And my only playmate was my sister, Cindy (she won't let me call her my little sister any longer, but she was definitely my little sister in those days—by three and a half years).

So when Marisa Carroll, Ellen James and I started discussing a trilogy about three sisters, the first thing I thought of was Florida's Gulf Coast.

The next thing I thought of was how I idolized my sister. To me, Cindy was as pretty as a princess. She had hair that fell to her waist—a lot like Amy's—and big brown eyes and fair skin that turned golden in the blazing Gulf Coast sun. She was smart and brave, and I was so proud of my little sister, I couldn't begin to express it.

I like writing about things that strike at the chords of our hearts—things like childhood memories and sisters. That's why I enjoyed working on the SISTERS trilogy so much— because while each sister discovers her one true love, she also finds a way back to what was lost in her relationships with her sisters. And what better place to do it than along Florida's Gulf Coast.

Enjoy!

*Peg Sutherland*

# Peg Sutherland

*Amy*

## Harlequin Books

TORONTO • NEW YORK • LONDON
AMSTERDAM • PARIS • SYDNEY • HAMBURG
STOCKHOLM • ATHENS • TOKYO • MILAN
MADRID • WARSAW • BUDAPEST • AUCKLAND

If you purchased this book without a cover you should be aware that this book is stolen property. It was reported as "unsold and destroyed" to the publisher, and neither the author nor the publisher has received any payment for this "stripped book."

ISBN 0-373-70734-7

AMY

Copyright © 1997 by Peg Robarchek.

All rights reserved. Except for use in any review, the reproduction or utilization of this work in whole or in part in any form by any electronic, mechanical or other means, now known or hereafter invented, including xerography, photocopying and recording, or in any information storage or retrieval system, is forbidden without the written permission of the publisher, Harlequin Enterprises Limited, 225 Duncan Mill Road, Don Mills, Ontario, Canada M3B 3K9.

All characters in this book have no existence outside the imagination of the author and have no relation whatsoever to anyone bearing the same name or names. They are not even distantly inspired by any individual known or unknown to the author, and all incidents are pure invention.

This edition published by arrangement with Harlequin Books S.A.

® and TM are trademarks of the publisher. Trademarks indicated with ® are registered in the United States Patent and Trademark Office, the Canadian Trade Marks Office and in other countries.

Printed in U.S.A.

*Amy*

## PROLOGUE

"MERRICK, I THINK WE should get a divorce."

Helene had lowered her voice, no doubt so that the housekeeper wouldn't overhear as she scurried around in the kitchen. Merrick thought surely he had misunderstood; perhaps he needed that hearing aid after all.

But no, Helene's smile was strained and her lovely eyes were troubled. And despite almost fifty years of marriage, that troubled Merrick.

"I'm not sure I heard that," he said, dabbing at the corners of his silver mustache with a linen napkin. "Could you tell me again what it is you have in mind, my dear?"

Helene looked at him uncertainly over her copy of the *Hurricane Beach Chronicle,* parts of which were scattered untidily over the rest of the table. Her eyes shone brightly, almost the same clear aqua as the waters of the Gulf of Mexico, which rose and fell over her shoulder. Her soft hair matched the frothy whitecaps in both color and pleasing disarray. Merrick marveled, as often he had over the past five decades, that this fascinating and gifted woman had chosen him.

"Well, not a real divorce," she said. "Sort of a faux divorce."

A faux divorce. As if that made more sense.

Helene had been the center of Merrick's life since he'd met her at a USO shindig during the chaos of World War II. She'd been singing "Don't Sit Under the Apple Tree with Anyone Else But Me," and Merrick had known immediately that this curvy strawberry blonde was the answer to his every dream.

Nothing meant as much to him as Helene. Not the fortune he'd managed to amass during his seventy-five years—although that was a considerable achievement given his humble beginnings as the son of a London merchant with no head for business. Not Sea Haven, the breathtaking coastal home where he and his wife had raised three lovely daughters. Not even the trim physique he maintained with his brisk daily walks along his private stretch of Hurricane Beach.

Certainly, Merrick was grateful for everything he had. But the one thing he valued above all was Helene.

Even talk of a faux divorce sent his blood pressure up a notch or two.

Merrick folded the front section of the *Wall Street Journal,* placed it carefully between the crystal glass of freshly squeezed juice and the china cup of imported coffee—special-ordered by that little shop on Gulfview Lane—and peered at Helene.

"To what purpose, my dear?" Merrick asked calmly.

Helene pursed her lips—a definite signal that Merrick had committed some error in judgment—and reached across the table to confiscate his neatly folded copy of the *Wall Street Journal.* "You haven't been listening, Merrick."

"Guilty as charged."

She drew a long breath. "What I'm trying to say, Merrick, is that I only want one thing for our fiftieth anniversary. I want a reconciliation between our girls."

Merrick sighed. If he'd had a clue how to accomplish a closeness between Lisa, Amy and Megan, he would have done so a dozen years ago. "Now, Helene, it isn't as if they're actually feuding."

The hurt in his wife's eyes stopped him cold. No rationalizations would do this morning, apparently.

"They hardly speak," she said. "Amy barely remembers which state Megan lives in and Megan changes the subject every time I mention Amy. And I can't remember the last time Lisa came home to see any of us."

Merrick frowned. Megan's estrangement at least they all understood. Losing a child would traumatize anyone. Who wouldn't want to stay away from the place where those distressing memories originated? Why, Merrick himself had found it impossible after World War II to return to London, where his family, his neighborhood, everything he'd known in life had been destroyed. Yes, Merrick understood his oldest daughter's reluctance to return to a place that held such painful reminders.

For a long time they had all expected Megan to come back into the fold for comfort. It hadn't happened.

And for that, Merrick knew, Helene blamed herself. As she blamed herself for the way Lisa had drifted off, and for Amy's capricious outlook on life. Merrick believed his three daughters were adults now, and responsible for themselves. But Helene believed the flaws in their lives were a reflection of her imperfection as a mother.

"Helene, my love, it isn't your fault," he said for what seemed like the millionth time. "And you must know there's nothing we can do."

"I think there is. But you'll have to go along with me."

So he heard her out. Then he told her no, in no uncertain terms. He had every reason to suppose that would be the end of it. After all, Merrick was the man of the house and in his day the man of the house made the decisions.

He had expected she might pout or give him the cold shoulder. But she was cordial and sweet the rest of the day. Cordial, sweet…and persistent.

After breakfast, she followed him into his study when he went to check for E-mail from his financial consultants, and went through the entire plan again. She talked of nothing else when they sat on the screened deck for lunch. She bombarded him with the pros and cons of her plan during their brisk walk along the beach at sunset. She served it up with cocktails before dinner.

Merrick kept telling himself he'd never allowed himself to be nagged into doing anything in his life. Then it occurred to him that Helene had never done anything that could even remotely be considered nagging.

"This is truly important to you, isn't it?" he said as he pulled her chair out at the dinner table.

She looked up at him over her shoulder, pleading in her eyes. "Yes, it is."

He sat across from her and poured the white wine. "You honestly believe that if we lead the girls to believe our marriage is in jeopardy, it will somehow pull them together."

"We can think of it as our own personal little play, Merrick. A chance to perform again."

Merrick frowned. He hadn't acted in forty years or more—not since he'd turned his back on the early days of TV. He'd been successful, certainly, but he'd never taken it as seriously as Helene. In fact, he'd followed his stagestruck bride to an audition, strictly as a lark, and ended up with a bit part on Broadway. One thing led to another and he'd eventually landed a TV series of his own. But he'd left it behind without a qualm when Helene had finally gotten pregnant. A normal life for their children, they'd agreed. Helene had been active, over the years, in the local community theater. Had even coaxed Merrick on stage once or twice. But this...

It made no sense at all to Merrick. But he loved Helene more deeply now than ever.

"My dear, I am yours to command," he said, raising his wineglass. He saw her eyes brighten as she raised her glass and touched it lightly to his. "Let the curtain rise."

# CHAPTER ONE

*HOW THE MIGHTY HAVE FALLEN.*

Yesterday, Jon Costas had been up to his neck in Wall Street sharks. This morning, he was up to his elbows in flour. He reminded himself the choice had been his.

More or less.

"I'm not sure I'm the best one to—"

His protest died when his *thea* Aurelia gave him the Look. Jon had cowered under his aunt's Look since he'd been caught snitching *koulourakia* cookies from the glass case at age six. Since the day he and his cousin Jimmy had decided to replace all the cinnamon at the family bakery with dirt. It was his uncle Nikos who'd caught them. But it was Aurelia and Jon's mother, Leda, who had given them the Look.

Greek matriarchs were masters of the Look, and used it most effectively to keep their men in line while still perpetuating the myth that the men were the ones in charge. At least, that was Jon's theory.

"Okay, okay," he said. "It's time I learned."

The Look softened and his *thea* Aurelia smiled. "That's my boy."

Wondering what his fellow sharks on Wall Street
would think if they could see him now, Jon plunged
his hands into the giant mound of bread dough on
the polished steel work counter and began to knead.
Thea Aurelia nodded, satisfied. Theo Nikos broke
into a wry grin without looking up from the fresh
spices he was grinding for the day's work.

"Knead like you take the head off that worthless
brother of yours," Aurelia coached, keeping a careful eye on him even as she checked the oven tem-
perature and pulled clean baking pans from the dish-
washer. "Give him the real going-over."

That wasn't too hard. Nick was the reason Jon
was here in the first place. Jon wouldn't have
minded giving his big brother a real going-over.

Not that Jon had been entirely happy with things
in New York. Life as a junior partner in a small but
prestigious brokerage company was stressful and
Wall Street was a jungle, to be sure. Certainly there
had been times when Jon had thought of chucking
it all, walking out and never looking back. Especially times like the day Malika had broken their
engagement, berating Jon for having no time for
anything but the ups and downs of the New York
Stock Exchange. That day might not have hurt as
much as it did, if it hadn't come two years to the
day after Katrina returned the exact ring, with almost the exact words.

He'd wondered if the two women had met somewhere.

Maybe, but only if they'd also run into Lisa somewhere along the way. Lisa's complaints had been very similar when she'd filed for divorce all those years ago.

So maybe, at thirty-five, it was time to quit Wall Street. He'd said as much to Bailey Bookman, the other junior partner and his most frequent comrade in the grim world of the New York singles scene.

Bailey, who'd gained fifteen pounds since making partner and took blood-pressure medication whenever he remembered it, had given Jon a skeptical look. "This is the broken engagement, isn't it?"

"No," Jon had said. "Well, maybe. A little. But mostly I'm sick of all this."

He'd waved his arm and Bailey had followed the gesture as it swept Jon's comfortable, if not yet opulent, office. "Which is the part you're sick of?" Bailey had asked. "The money? The prestige? Or maybe it's just the promise of more of the same that's weighing you down."

"How about the heartburn and the blood pressure and the realization that I've got no life."

Then it had been Bailey's turn to wave his hand dismissively. "Having a life is way overrated. You get a life, you just end up paying another divorce attorney."

"I'm going, Book. I told you a year ago I was thinking about it."

"A year ago you were talking a fishing boat in the Keys. A little financial consulting on the side.

Now you're talking a *bakery?* Come on, Costas.
You're not escaping, you're being shanghaied.''

"It's not like it's forever," Jon had said. "Six
months."

"They'll get their hooks into you. You'll never
get away."

The challenge had stirred unease in Jon. His family had pressured him to come back since his brother
had abandoned the family business and his teenage
daughter. But Jon wasn't about to explain that to
Book. "Six months. I'll be back."

Jon had repeated that promise a dozen times his
last week in New York. Because Bailey was right,
of course. When Jon had spoken of getting out of
Wall Street, he'd had in mind something free and
easy. No family to tie him down, no aunts and uncles looking over his shoulder, no Mama and Pop
hoping he would fulfill the expectations their older
son had disappointed.

No, standing here kneading dough in the Costas
Family Bakery in Hurricane Beach, Florida, was not
Jon's idea of an alternative life-style.

*Thanks, Nick.*

If Wall Street was a jungle, Costas Family Bakery
wasn't exactly serenity park. A dozen people—all
family—scurried around this morning, shouting in a
hybrid of Greek and English, banging oven doors,
slamming refrigerator doors and clattering baking
pans and utensils. Already, Jon felt suffocated, and

a little panicky that so much was expected of him. *Six months,* he reassured himself. *Tops.*

"Still a madhouse, I see," Jon said to Nikos as Aurelia followed Leda, both women chattering like a runaway subway car.

Nikos shrugged. "I see the pictures from Wall Street in the paper. Not so bad here, maybe."

"Wall Street I understood."

Nikos grunted as he refilled the stainless steel canisters with fresh spices. "Here is not much to understand. Here, you do whatever is next and the work gets done and life goes on."

Jon sighed. Life, indeed, did go on in Hurricane Beach. Nothing had changed since he'd last worked here as a senior in high school. Thea Aurelia, flushed from the heat, still kept an eye on the ovens. Theo Nikos still ordered the younger generation hither and yon. Jon's pop, Demetri, reigned over the front of the shop—particularly the cash register— and his mother, Leda, handled packaging. In reality, however, nobody could keep his or her hands out of anybody else's territory and the result was noisy— if friendly—chaos. Jon had hated it when he'd worked here during his teens, had felt choked by the constant closeness. He had learned to view the place with a certain detached fondness when he came home for visits in the years since college. But now— especially now that every Costas in Hurricane Beach mistakenly viewed him as the patriarch-in-training—Jon imagined he would grow to hate it again, in very short order.

*No wonder Nick drugged himself into oblivion.*

The chaos reached its height as the time neared eight, when the front doors would officially open for the morning traffic and the trucks began to roll with deliveries to restaurants and small markets up and down the Florida panhandle. Theo Nikos was yelling and Thea Aurelia was slamming oven doors and Leda was bemoaning the state of Jon's latest batch of yeasty dough.

"Oh, no, no, no," she complained, crossing herself before she took over the lump of dough herself. "Is all wrong."

Aurelia peered over her sister-in-law's shoulder. "Is all right."

"Is overworked already! Hopeless!"

Aurelia snatched it away from Leda. "Can't be."

Jon stood there with sticky white hands, wondering why it was that everyone insisted he start his first day on the job by baking. "Maybe I should just wash up and go help Dad with—"

"You stay put," Leda said.

And from Aurelia, the Look.

A soft, breathy voice over his shoulder said, "I'd follow orders if I were you."

Something familiar about the voice gave Jon a momentary flutter of unease. This was not his sister, not one of his cousins nor a niece. And yet.

He glanced over his shoulder and the flutter of unease cranked up into full-fledged consternation.

"Amy."

She smiled, the smile of childlike delight that had always been a trademark of those Hardaway girls. "You remember."

Of course he remembered Amy. The Hardaway girls had haunted him all through adolescence, beautiful and friendly and way out of reach for the working-class son of immigrant shop owners. They were the stuff that dreams were made of for every teenage boy in Hurricane Beach. Until college, when rebellion and loneliness had driven one of them right into his arms. Lisa, the cool one.

He'd married her, and the dreams had faded.

Lisa Hardaway had been Jon's biggest failure. The deal he'd clinched only to have it go sour. He'd done a pretty good job of putting his marriage out of his mind the last several years. And when he'd reluctantly agreed to come home to help the family straighten out the mess Nick had left behind, Jon hadn't expected constant reminders to be a problem. Everyone in the Costas family, at one time or another, had assured him that his ex-wife rarely came back to Hurricane Beach.

And now, here was Amy, his ex-sister-in-law. Amy, who shouldn't be a problem. After all, she was nothing like Lisa. Even after all these years, Amy had the look of a woodland sprite. Her long strawberry-blond hair fell past her shoulders, clipped back with plastic barrettes—the kind little girls wear, painted with the face of a clown. Soft frizz, coaxed out by the humidity of a Florida spring, wafted at her temples. A gauzy dress floated over her slender body, ending almost at her ankles. A chain of tiny gold shells encircled one of those ankles. Bare toes, painted a soft lavender, peeked out from strappy little sandals.

No, Amy in no way reminded him of his ex-wife. So that should be no problem at all. Except...

"What are you doing here?" he asked, a glance at the big industrial clock on the wall telling him the shop wasn't yet officially open to the public. Family only, before and after hours. That had always been the rule.

Her bright smile wavered. He'd spoken too sharply. A small taste of his old guilt came back.

Before she could answer, Aurelia spotted Amy and let out a shrill cry of welcome.

Jon cringed as his aunt enveloped tall, slender Amy in a crushing hug. They were treating her like family. Hell, they'd never even greeted Lisa that warmly, and she *had* been family. What was he doing here, for goodness' sake?

*You owe me, Nick. Big time.*

AMY STUCK her hand in the bakery case and used fresh tissue to retrieve almond rolls for her paper bag, as she did every morning before walking two doors down to unlock Rêve Rags. This morning, however, she felt self-conscious about the familiar routine. Her fingers quivered, mimicking the way her insides felt. Was he watching?

"So, we have to get all the money off his hands before he makes a baker, eh?" Aurelia nudged her, speaking loudly enough for others to hear.

Folding the top of her bag, Amy grinned and glanced toward the back. Jon Costas stood in the open doorway, gazing at her in that way she'd never been able to fathom. Never, not twenty years ago when he'd caused her first adolescent heartbreak, and not now. Inscrutable, his feelings hidden behind those eyes the color of coffee untouched by even a dollop of cream. Bottomless brown. He'd been like that as long as she could remember, from the first time she'd noticed him in junior high.

What, she wondered, could it have been like to be married to him?

She pushed the thought away. It was one she'd had before. She certainly didn't intend to entertain it again.

"There's only one way he's going to make a baker," she said lightly, digging through the woven purse slung over her shoulder for money to cover her purchase. "He needs an apron."

"Aha!" Aurelia wagged a finger at her nephew. "What did I say? This boy needs an apron. Didn't I say that, Leda, not two hours ago?"

Jon folded his arms across his chest, apparently forgetting he was still covered to his elbows with flour and clumps of drying dough. He looked down and frowned. His navy T-shirt was already liberally dusted with flour. "I do not need an apron."

Aurelia shrugged. Amy replied with an answering shrug.

"Maybe he isn't meant to be a baker," Amy said, suppressing her grin. "Maybe he needs to go out on the boats."

Aurelia's sons operated the most successful fishing fleet in the gulf, supplying local restaurants and fish markets with the day's fresh catch. Amy had dated Jimmy, the oldest, for six months, but the scent of grouper and shrimp that clung to him so tenaciously had threatened to rob her of her love of seafood.

Besides, Jimmy's kisses had been polite and sweet and Amy had told herself she had time to hold out for something more. Love should feel like a hurricane taking possession of her body, shouldn't it? Amy had decided to wait it out and Jimmy was married now, to a lovely young Greek woman from New Jersey whose father knew Jimmy's father, Nikos, from the old country.

Still not sorry for the lost opportunity, Amy turned to Aurelia. "What do you say, Thea Aurelia? Maybe you ought to send him out with Jimmy."

"To the boats?" Aurelia looked aghast. "Oh, no, this boy is not for the boats. Look at these hands."

"Aurelia," Jon protested, but it was pointless to

resist. Aurelia had already taken him by one hand and dragged him over to Amy.

"Look at these fingers. Long and slender. Hands for kneading."

Amy studied the white hands offered up for inspection. They were, indeed, the hands of a man who ought to be doing something very manual yet something very delicate.

"Nick," Aurelia continued, "he never had these hands. No, Jon is for the bakery. It is for sure."

Amy frowned as if in doubt and took Jon's hand in hers, turned it over and examined the other side. Perhaps he would smile. Surely, in this big, boisterous Costas family a smile was genetically unavoidable. "You're sure? I don't know, maybe the palms are a little tough. He could flatten the yeast that way, you know."

Aurelia waved at her in disgust. "Hah! Flatten the yeast. You American! No Greek in your blood, this much is for sure. Even a little bit of good Greek blood and never would you say such a foolish thing."

Then she walked off, calling out to her husband to check the number-two oven, and left Amy standing there with Jon.

"So, you've come home," she said, dropping his hand, which truly didn't look the least bit tough.

"Well, for now, at least."

"I know what you mean," she said, hoping to set him at ease. "I used to think once I was out of here,

I was gone for good. But when I finally left, I couldn't wait to finish college and get home."

He nodded, looking back at the raucous interaction coming from the baking room. Well, so much for captivating him with her charm, wit and understanding.

"It was good of you to come," she said. "Not everyone would."

"That's me," he said wryly. "Model son Jon Costas."

"You're bitter," she said, once again reading things into what he hadn't said. "About Nick."

She recognized the look he gave her and immediately knew she'd crossed the line between friendly interest and downright nosiness.

"Sorry." She smiled sheepishly. "I tend to forget some things are none of my business. Even with family."

"Family?"

Apparently he didn't think of her as family anymore.

"Well, formerly family." She shrugged. "Guess I'll let you get back to it."

When he nodded, she turned, punched the cash register, deposited her money and retrieved her change, dropped it into her enormous purse and turned to go. He was still staring at her with the unreadable gaze that had always disconcerted her. Even when he'd been married to her sister.

Now *there* was a pair, she thought. Lisa made her uneasy these days, too.

"Later," she said cheerily, still angling for a smile.

No such luck. Too bad. If memory served, Jon Costas had the kind of smile that curled hair.

Lisa didn't smile much, either, these days.

Amy left by the back door, contemplating the discontent in Jon Costas. What would it take, she wondered, to make him smile?

She had just turned the key to her shop when the answer came to her.

*Lisa.* Lisa, who also needed a reason to smile.

# CHAPTER TWO

BY THE TIME her partner arrived, Amy could barely contain herself.

"I have a plan," she said, ushering Grace King-solver in and closing the shop door behind her.

"Uh-oh," Grace said as she walked to the back room to stash her purse. "Amy has a plan. Words to strike terror into the hearts of sane people the world over."

Amy hoisted herself onto the little shop's check-out counter and waited for Grace to return to the front of the store. She dangled her feet impatiently, staring at herself in the wall of mirrors across from her. It pleased her to note that she looked almost as if she were perched on the acrylic pier that was part of the mural she and her art students—kids from YMCA—had painted on the wall behind her.

Grace dragged a rack of newly consigned spring dresses out from the back room. She looked at her partner skeptically, her brown eyes almost the same shade as her skin, coffee barely touched with cream.

"Really, this one is a good idea," Amy said, pro-testing the message in her partner's gaze as Grace began to rack the dresses by size. "I'm going to help Lisa patch things up with Jon."

Grace closed her eyes in what Amy interpreted as a silent plea for patience. "Girl, you've lost your mind. You know that, don't you?"

"No, I haven't. If you'd seen him just now—"

"You didn't share this little brainstorm with him, I hope."

Amy rolled her eyes. "Well, I should hope not."

"Thank you, God, for small favors."

"If you'll just listen for a—"

Grace pointed at the clock. "Time to open up."

Amy slid off the counter and unlocked the front door, but not before making a face at her partner. In college, Grace had been as daring as her roommate. Together, they had masterminded the plan to run one of Grace's boyfriends for homecoming queen—and managed to secure the crown for him. They had launched a campaign to make the campus more accessible for disabled students and had spent one summer building houses for the homeless in Central America. Opening their funky little shop in Hurricane Beach had seemed like the biggest adventure of all.

But they were older now. Both 34 to be exact, and over the years, especially in the ten years since they'd opened their consignment shop, Grace had changed. Amy hated to even think it, but sometimes it seemed to her that Grace had committed the unpardonable. Grace had grown up.

Well, Amy had no plans to give in to the pressure.

"Let me know when you can't stand the suspense anymore and I'll tell you the rest of my plan," she said, all dignity as she propped their door open with their plaster guard dog, Killer.

She would have sworn Grace mumbled something about not holding her breath as they went about racking the rest of the spring clothes. Winter stock went onto the rolling rack and would be marked down and displayed on the sidewalk, beginning next weekend.

Amy managed to keep quiet until Grace found the bakery bag on the counter and took out her almond roll.

"They're both miserable," Amy offered, bringing coffee in Disney mugs from the back.

Grace raised one of her perfect eyebrows. "They tell you this? Or are you reading minds again?"

"Jon doesn't even want to be here," Amy said. "His cousin Jimmy told me that. If it weren't for that sorry brother of his—"

Grace looked away.

"Oh, God, I'm sorry, Grace. I talk too much."

Grace smiled faintly. "No need to apologize. I won't break."

No doubt that was true, because if Grace were the breaking kind, Nick Costas's disappearance a month ago would no doubt have done the job. Amy had worried about the relationship between Grace and Nick, knowing Nick had a troublesome history with drugs. But the attraction between the two had been too strong.

Nick had been in and out of treatment for his addictions most of his adult life. But when he'd survived his wife's death five years ago without a relapse, everyone in town pronounced him cured. He'd taken over most of the responsibility for the family bakery. He'd seemed to be a good father to Kieran, his teenage dauᵧhter. Gradually, however, Nick had rediscovered his love for drugs, a dependence that was more powerful, apparently, than his love for Grace. More powerful, even, than his love for his own daughter.

At Grace's urging, he'd made it to rehab, but he'd lasted only three days before walking out in the middle of the night. No one had seen him since.

"Nick left a real mess behind," Grace said softly. "Who could blame Jon if he doesn't like having to come in and clean up after his big brother? But that doesn't mean he wants his ex-wife back, you know."

Amy ignored that. Of course he would want Lisa back. Who wouldn't want Lisa back? Perfect, capable Lisa. And as far as Lisa wanting Jon back, well, she had seen the man up close this morning. That chiseled face, with the faintest of fine lines around his eyes. Those eyes. Those square shoulders. Those arms. Those hands. Even that hair, short and crisp and prematurely the color of new silver, flattering his dark Mediterranean complexion. Jon Costas was a man to die for and—

*Enough of that.*

"Anyway, all I need is a way to get Lisa back to Hurricane Beach for a while."

"That's a trick I can't wait to see, considering your sister hasn't been back here for more than a day at a time in years."

"Leave it to me," Amy said, licking sugary crumbs off her fingers as two women paused on the sidewalk, considering the window display, then came through the door.

"What I want to know," Grace whispered as she headed off to greet the customers, "is what *really* put this idea in your head to start with."

Amy cleared away their morning snack while Grace directed the two women to their sizes and recommended a line of hand-painted vests the store carried on consignment from a local artist. Her partner's question nagged her. She knew what put this idea in her head, but it wasn't something she was willing to discuss, even with her best friend.

When she'd first heard the news that her former brother-in-law was coming back to Hurricane Beach, Amy had felt an alarmingly familiar tug.

The first time she'd felt that particular sensation was her first day at junior high, a lowly seventh-grader, awkward and unsure of herself. Walking up the cracked, buckling sidewalk, eyes on the enormous school that drew kids from two surrounding counties, Amy had prayed for the ground to swallow her up.

For a moment, it appeared that her prayer had been answered. The sidewalk came up to meet her. Her books went flying. And all she was aware of were stinging knees and the guffaws of the others around her. For a moment, she was paralyzed, certain now that she would never be able to face these older kids. Even Megan, her older sister, would surely disavow any relationship with this long-legged goon who couldn't even walk straight.

Then someone sat beside her on the sidewalk. She couldn't even look up to see who. She began scrabbling her books back together again. A big, warm hand landed on her arm and a quiet voice said, "You okay?"

Blinking back the moisture in her eyes, she'd looked up into the face of Jon Costas. She remembered him from elementary school. She remembered him from the bakery on Gulfview, where her mom sent her or one of her sisters for fresh bread every couple of days.

"Sure," she mumbled.

"Good."

He smiled at her. The most incredible smile she'd ever seen. His teeth were straight and white against his dark skin—he would never need braces like the ones the dentist had already sentenced her to. And where his hand touched her arm, she began to tingle.

She thought at first he must have felt it too, because he removed his hand at that very instant. He started helping her pick up her books, and pretended not to notice that she had skinned both her knees.

"Welcome to Coastal Junior High," he'd said, handing her the books and smiling again. Then he'd backed away and left her standing there, knees skinned, self-confidence bruised, but her female instincts newly blossoming.

Amy had fancied herself in love with Jon Costas for the next two school years, until he'd gone off to high school. By the time she made it to high school herself, Amy was mature enough to realize that mooning after Jon Costas was an exercise in futility.

Then, years later, he had walked through the front door of her parents' house on Lisa's arm. Despite the ceilings in the great room at Sea Haven and the large windows overlooking a pristine expanse of white silver sands and turquoise gulf, Amy had suddenly felt boxed in. She'd spent the next two years denying the tug she felt whenever she was around Jon. She'd been grateful Lisa and Jon rarely showed their faces in Hurricane Beach in those days. When her sister's marriage hit the rocks, Jon Costas was out of Amy's life for good. Or so she'd thought. She certainly never expected he'd come back to Hurricane Beach.

She'd apparently underestimated the pull of his family.

Or hers, for that matter. The pull of family was precisely what had drawn her back to Hurricane

Beach after college—she'd hoped for a return to that perfect time in her life—the time when she and her sisters had been the best of friends. Before things had gone awry.

So far, it hadn't happened, but she still clung to the fantasy of making everything all right.

Thank goodness for her parents and their unwavering dedication. Without them, Amy knew, she would feel more adrift than she sometimes did. Helene and Merrick Hardaway held it together for her, kept her from feeling quite so abandoned by her sisters, both of whom wanted little to do with the family in Hurricane Beach.

But with the return of Jon Costas, Amy saw a possibility for recapturing at least a part of what had been lost. And as a fringe benefit, she might even get over some of her guilt over the way she'd once felt about Jon.

THE MONTHLY MEETING of the Hurricane Beach Merchants' Association droned on for what seemed like hours as people discussed plans for Spring Break events. Jon checked his watch. He'd been here thirty minutes so far.

His seat at the meeting was yet another little item he'd inherited by default when his brother had disappeared. As soon as he'd walked in—having showered away every sign of flour and yeast and sugar—he'd been amazed how many of these people he still remembered from a dozen years ago.

There was stout and balding Ike Forenza from the open-air Italian café, stout and bushy-haired Glenda Hendricks from the resort-wear boutique, Maida-with-no-last-name from the art gallery and Quentin Somersby the florist.

And—he might have known—Amy Hardaway.

She'd smiled and waved when he came in, gesturing to an empty seat on her left. But he'd moved to the other end of the table, taking a seat between Quentin and old man Thompson from the pharmacy.

Jon realized that most of these folks had changed no more than the town itself. Maida had a different little dog tucked into her oversize tote bag, and Ike's hairline had receded all the way to his crown. Bea Connell, whose family owned the brass foundry, had aged more than the years called for. But Jon recalled that she'd lost most of her family in a plane crash, so the air of fragility about her was to be expected.

Otherwise, everything looked the same. Gulfview Lane still ran for three blocks, its shops fronted by a broad sidewalk running parallel to the beach. On the street behind Gulfview, a row of Victorian cottages were elaborately painted in pastels. The marina and yacht club anchored one end and a fishing pier the other. Beyond the pier to the east, the stretch of flat, wide beach went on for miles. On the west end of Gulfview Lane, the beach began a gradual curve to create Alligator Bay. Where Alligator Creek, a branch of the Apalachicola River, spilled into the gulf, the water became deep enough to accommodate a wharf for fishing boats and a marina. The terrain was different there. Instead of low, flat beaches with their sea oats and pennywort, there were slash pines and palmetto and live oaks.

In between the marsh-like forest at the bay and the pristine beaches beyond the pier, the little town perched. Along Gulfview, dozens of prosperous, upscale shops—a bookstore, a fresh seafood market, a grocer, a pharmacy, two gift shops specializing in tasteful seashore memorabilia—catered both to locals and to a small but loyal tourist community.

Tucked into the bend of the Gulf of Mexico, the little town of Hurricane Beach managed to avoid the kind of tourism that had overwhelmed so many of the cities and towns along Florida's Gold Coast. There were no hotels or motels, only a few discreet bed-and-breakfast inns, and a row of rental cabins along the beach. Most of the tourists who came to Hurricane Beach—swelling its population to almost ten thousand during the season—owned their own cottages. College students had not discovered Hurricane Beach and would have found nothing to keep them coming back if they had. There were no water slides and no miniature-golf courses, no nightclubs with strobe lights and deafening music.

And everybody in Hurricane Beach liked it that way. Some said it was the desire to isolate that had led the founding fathers to choose the town's name in the first place. Jon suspected that story was nothing but local lore.

Out of sheer boredom, and in hopes of encouraging others to get moving so they could get this interminable meeting over with, Jon volunteered to head up the fireworks committee, accepting responsibility for the grand finale of Spring Break, which this year fell on the first week in April.

After an hour, people on both sides of the table began to shuffle, and Jon had hopes the movement signaled the end of the meeting. All it signaled, as it turned out, was a break so everyone could refill coffee cups.

He remained seated. He knew he should mingle, reacquaint himself with these people, force himself to act friendly and glad to be here. But right at this moment, he didn't feel he was that good an actor. He wasn't glad to be here, in this meeting or in Hurricane Beach. He didn't want to spend the rest of his life kneading dough and playing father to a sullen teenager.

His niece's fifteenth birthday celebration had been Sunday. Lots of home-baked goodies, a little music, cousins and nieces and nephews coming out of the woodwork. A pile of brightly wrapped gifts had covered the oak dining table in the house where he'd grown up. The house where he was presently living, with his mother, his father and his brother's daughter.

Kieran had barely surfaced all day. Long enough to eat cake and make faces at the *dolmades* and souvlaki. Long enough to open presents, most of which she'd looked at with a lack of enthusiasm bordering on insolence. She'd spent much of the day locked in her bedroom, in front of that damn computer his brother had bought her. Jon could read the motivation behind that particular little bit of generosity. Give the kid a computer and access to the Internet, and she'd be off his back, leaving Nick with plenty of time for his own favorite playtime activity.

*Nick, you sorry jerk.*

Jon told himself he was spending entirely too much time talking to his vanished-into-thin-air brother.

He was about to drag himself out of his chair and into the fray of friendliness, when someone sat on the table and looked down at him. Amy.

*Damn.*

"So, did you ever get it right? The kneading, I mean?"

She was grinning at him. He tried to decide, for a moment, which was deeper, the dimple in her cheek or the one in her chin.

"I don't think I'm in any danger of having Betty Crocker ask my advice," he said, trying for civility. No reason to take it out on Amy Hardaway just because his life was temporarily offtrack.

It struck him, then, that she might no longer be Amy Hardaway. How many years had it been since he'd seen her? Six? Eight? Hell, he'd been engaged twice, so why would he assume she hadn't managed to find Mr. Right.

He tried to catch a glimpse of her ring finger, but she was sitting on her hands. A row of golden bangles tinkled against the table. The batik pants she wore were soft and loose, tied with a big sash at the waist. Her long hair floated around her shoulders. Had it always been that particular shade of sand and ginger? he wondered. Her eyes that spectacular shade of pale sea green?

In his memory, the Hardaway girls had always looked remarkably alike. But seeing her again, Jon realized that Amy looked very little like Lisa. And it was more than the fact that his serious, subdued Lisa would never wear those pants, would never grow her hair halfway down her back and let it fly loose that way. No, Amy had a little-girl gleam in her eyes that he'd never seen in Lisa's.

He realized he'd never seen it in any of the serious, driven women he always chose to date. It suited Amy.

"Baking is an art, you know," Amy said. "I never could bake. Now, Lisa, *she* could bake."

"She could?"

Amy nodded. "Lisa is a wonder. I guess you know how well she's doing. I mean, I suppose you stay in touch. Since there was no real animosity when you split."

The last thing Jon wanted to talk about was his ex-wife. He stood. "I think I'll have some coffee."

She hopped off the table. She could almost look him squarely in the eye. He'd forgotten how tall she was, the tallest of the sisters, if he recalled.

"It's decaf," she said. "It'll never keep you awake. I always load up before I get here. So there you have it, an insider's tip. Illegal, I know. But you won't turn me in, will you?"

He grinned. And before he knew what was happening, she had grasped his arm. "I knew I could do it! A smile! Wow! Thanks. You still have a terrific smile, did you know that?"

He never intended it, but he laughed at the delight on her face. None of the people he knew anymore would be so transparent in their pleasure. The game as he knew it today was about control—keeping one's feelings in check. Apparently, Amy wasn't aware of that. "No, I didn't know."

"Sure, I'll bet you did," she said, trailing after him to the coffee table. "Why, I'll bet Lisa told you plenty of times."

"Listen, about Lisa—"

"Oh, she's doing so well. I guess you know about her group home for pregnant teens. Isn't it wonderful? I mean, dedicating your life to making a difference for others. I'm so in awe of what she does."

He poured coffee, hoping someone else would interrupt Amy's monologue about his ex-wife. She kept it up all the way back to the table—the count-less lives Lisa had touched, heck, she must be up for sainthood, to hear Amy tell it—and he'd just about decided that he was going to have to tell her straight out to put a lid on it, when the meeting resumed.

Saved.

Or so he thought. The last item on the agenda was to fill the positions on each committee. Amy volunteered for fireworks detail. She was the only one. From her seat at the other end of the table, she leaned forward and waggled her fingers at him, that impish smile stoking his frustration.

Once the meeting broke up, Jon tried to get away without having to talk to Amy. Not that he didn't love being reminded what a miserable failure he'd made of his marriage to the perfect Lisa, he thought with irony. But by the time he reached the sidewalk in front of the bank, he heard her calling after him.

"Wait up," she said. "I'll walk partway with you."

How rude would it be to say no thanks? he wondered. In New York, he wouldn't have had to ask himself that question. In New York, rude was everybody's favorite hobby.

He decided, instead, to waylay her before she got started on more "My Sister, the Saint" stories.

"So, tell me what you've been doing all these

years," he said, shoving his hands into his pants pockets.

It worked. She launched into another running monologue. He could barely keep up with the stories about houses for the homeless and street art along Jackson Square in New Orleans. There was no mention of a husband.

"You'll have to come see our shop," she said. "Rêve Rags. My college roommate and I opened it about ten years ago."

"Grace."

She glanced at him but he didn't glance back.

"I guess you know about Grace," she said.

"Yeah. I know about Grace." Another of his brother's messy little problems. Despite it all, Jon was hit with a wave of sorrow. Dammit, he missed his brother. At least, he missed the brother he'd once had, before drugs had worked their black magic on him.

Jon thought, as he had more than once, that he might have been able to make a difference. Might have been able to say just the right thing to make Nick see the light, even though all the experts on addiction said it didn't work that way. Still, Jon's heart ached that he'd never taken the time to find out. He'd been too busy trying to get away himself.

"It was Grace's idea," Amy was saying. "The store, I mean. We do consignments. Designer clothes. Handmade things from some of the artist colonies along the coast. You know, jewelry and weaving, things like that. We have painted silk sarongs that would leave you breathless. I'm not kidding."

"I'll drop in sometime and have a look," he said, more to be polite than anything.

"We have a little silver and gold cocktail number that would go great with your coloring," she said.

At the saucy way she said it, he laughed. Again. He liked her teasing manner, he realized. Amy was fun, when she wasn't harping on Lisa.

Oh, yeah. Lisa.

"It'll work out, you know," she said as they rounded the corner to his block. "It'll be an adjustment, of course. But in six months you'll wake up one morning and realize you're glad you're here and not in the city anymore."

He wanted to ask her what in the world made her think she knew him well enough to make such a prediction. But as he turned the corner and spotted the little white gate in front of his parents' house a block away, he realized he didn't care what her answer would be. He didn't want to listen to her, didn't want to get caught up in whatever positive, upbeat mind-set allowed Amy Hardaway to maintain such a bright, naive smile.

"I won't be here long enough for that," he said.

"Oh, really?"

He told himself he owed her no answers. "Uh-huh."

But Amy Hardaway, he was beginning to discover, was not easily dissuaded. "Why not?" she said.

He gave her a look. Maybe he'd watched his aunt Aurelia often enough that he could give it himself. Then again, maybe not. Amy seemed unfazed by the displeasure he'd meant to convey.

"You know, I never did believe you'd stick with that stock-market stuff when you and Lisa went up there."

"You didn't?" He hadn't meant to say that, either. But her observation surprised him and he'd opened his mouth before he realized what he was doing.

And that was apparently all the encouragement Amy needed. She shook her head. "You're too much a people person to play with toy money all day."

"It's not toy money," he said stiffly, even though he'd griped too often himself about the paper fortunes won and lost on Wall Street every day.

Again, Amy, breezed on, unfazed by his reaction. "Oh, I know what goes on up there is important. I don't *understand* it, exactly, but I know it's...vital. I mean, I could hardly have been around Dad all my life without knowing how important the stock market is. But you always seemed to be the kind of person who thought that people were more important. Than money, I mean.''

She paused for a breath and he tumbled a few disclaimers around in his head. But before he could reply, she said, "I know where I heard that. Lisa told me."

"Lisa?" Somehow, he couldn't imagine Lisa saying something like that about him. Not even in the early days when she might have thought such a thing. Lisa wasn't one for confiding in anyone, not even in her sisters.

"Oh, yes."

The way she said it sounded as though Lisa had spoken about him quite often. Quite intimately. The notion made him squirm inside.

"About Lisa…"

"Yes?"

What about her? Anything he might have to say about that relationship wouldn't be appropriate to share with her sister, anyway. He struggled for some safe comment, marveling that Amy had drawn him so far into this conversation. "I've always been sorry. About the way things happened." That much was true.

"Oh, I know it would help Lisa to hear that," she said.

Swell. Now Amy of the Nonstop Conversation could report back to Lisa.

"I'm sure she has regrets, too," Amy said.

Marrying him was probably number one on the list, he thought.

"Talking about things like this has always been hard on Lisa," Amy said. "We never were a hundred percent sure what happened between you two."

Jon was no fool. He'd already gone too far down this path with his ex-sister-in-law, but he at least knew when it was time to call a halt. "It was a long time ago."

There, he thought. That was enough to stop any normal person. But not Amy.

"But you didn't just stop loving her, or anything like that. Did you?"

He damn well had no intention of explaining that he and Lisa had probably never loved each other in the first place. Not the kind of grown-up love that was required to make a marriage work. "No," he said. "Nothing like that."

"Then what?"

He stopped at his front gate and looked at her, unsure what to say.

She grinned and said, "You just have to tell me it's none of my business. That's the only way to shut me up. According to Grace."

"Good night, Amy."

He walked up the sidewalk toward the house, resisting the urge to look back. Even when she called out, "But even that only works temporarily. I'm tenacious, too."

He laughed despite his irritation. "And I'm stubborn. Where does that leave us?"

"In a battle of wills?"

"Give it up, Hardaway. You're out of your league." But he was smiling as he said it.

She had the last laugh. But only for the moment, he told himself. Amy Hardaway wasn't family any longer and he didn't have to put up with her pesky persistence. Or the memories she brought with her.

# CHAPTER THREE

HELENE LIT the candles scattered around the great room, then double-checked to make sure each one stood straight in its holder. She reminded the house-keeper, Annie, for the third time, to give the wine plenty of time to breathe. She straightened the sea-scape watercolor Amy had painted five years ago for Merrick's seventieth birthday.

"You're nervous."

She jumped at the sound of Merrick's deep voice. "Oh, darling, you look splendid."

Then she walked across the room and tugged at the crisp collar of his shirt, as if her efforts could improve on perfection. Merrick was altogether the most handsome man she'd ever known, and she'd known plenty of good lookers when she and Merrick had been in show business. Deep of chest and broad of shoulder, he looked rugged to her, the kind of man you could depend on. He smiled, took her hand in his and kissed the tips of her fingers.

"I'm not nervous," she protested, following as he held her hand and led her to one of the half-dozen white wicker rockers lining their broad, oceanfront deck. "Why, it's only Amy for dinner. I just—"

"Want everything to be perfect," he finished for her.

She liked that, too, when he knew exactly what she was thinking before she even said.

He poured two small snifters of brandy from the decanter on the silver tray nearby and handed one to her.

"I know, my dear," he said. "You simply want a smooth opening night for our little performance."

Helene took the snifter, but wasn't sure she wanted it. She needed to be sharp tonight, didn't she? To stay on her toes. Or would things go better if she loosened up? Oh, heavens, why hadn't she taken that part in last fall's community-theater play, after all? She hadn't been on the stage in years; too many years, she realized.

"A case of stage fright isn't like you," Merrick said.

"I know," she said absently, running through her plan for the night in the same way she'd always run through her lines in those final moments before she took the stage. But this was more important than anything she'd done in her six years with the USO or her ten years on Broadway; more important, even, than Merrick's two years on TV.

"Funny, isn't it," she said, "that we gave up acting for the sake of our girls and now, here we are, acting again. For their sake."

"My dear—"

His words struck her and she snapped her fingers.

"And that's another thing," she told him. "I think you should guard against calling me 'dear.'"

He sat in the rocker beside her. She glanced at him and saw he still smiled.

"And you shouldn't smile so much, either," she added. "You know, Merrick, this isn't going to work if we seem too happy."

He sipped his brandy and gave her one of his devilish smiles, the kind that had captured her fancy when she'd first met him at a USO production during the war. "I suppose I'll have to hold off kissing your fingers, too."

"Or the back of my neck," she agreed, trying to remember all the little places he was prone to kiss during the course of a day. "Or on the forehead or certainly not on the..." She looked at him. "You're joshing me. Now, Merrick, I hope you won't forget how—"

"Serious you are about this. I won't forget." He set his snifter on the tray in front of them and leaned toward her. "I don't suppose I could have one last kiss to tide me over till our daughter leaves and I'm allowed to love my wife once again, could I?"

AMY CURLED in one of the rockers on the deck with a cup of cappuccino, as she always did after dinner with her parents, and let the sound of the surf wash over her. But tonight, it didn't soothe her.

Tonight, the raucous screeching of sea gulls overrode the lulling rhythm of the waves.

"Don't you think you've had enough?" Helene said as Merrick leaned forward to splash a little more brandy into his snifter.

The reproof gouged another hole in Amy's serenity. Never in her life could she remember her mother using that judgmental tone of voice with her father. And it had been like that all evening. Helene sounded disapproving, Merrick countered by sounding defensive. Helene's tone was sharp, Merrick's blustery.

Even in the dim light from the hurricane lamps bolted to the beams, Amy saw the frown deepening on her father's craggy face. "I think this has gone far enough. That's what I think."

She'd never heard quite that tone from him, either. At least not since she and her sisters were teens and one of them blew a curfew or brought home a speeding ticket. It was his stage voice, left over from his acting career, a deep, commanding voice that always called to mind her mother's scrapbook of their years as performers. Although Merrick Hardaway was always firm, clearly in command of his family, he'd rarely had to resort to that voice. And he'd never been harsh, especially with his wife. The uneasiness in Amy grew, tightening and hardening.

Tonight, perhaps, was not the night to float her trial balloon about Jon Costas. She'd counted on being able to mention him, to hint at her plan. Then, perhaps, Jon—and Lisa, of course—wouldn't occupy so much of her thoughts.

But the knot in her stomach told her this was not the night for talking of Jon.

"Now, Merrick," Helene said, "you promised."

"I never promised to be treated like a lush!"

His raised voice startled Amy so much that she dropped her cup, splashing the legs of the wicker rocker. The tinkle of shattering china barely broke the tension on the deck.

"Oh, gracious," Helene said, jumping up.

"Bloody hell!" Merrick bellowed. "Leave it be!"

Helene looked at him, the stunned expression on her face a mirror image of the disbelief in Amy's heart. *Please don't let this happen*, Amy thought. The idea of any kind of real conflict between her parents sent waves of anxiety rippling through her.

"Mom? Dad?" She looked from one to the other, from her mother's quivering lower lip, which Helene quickly clamped between her teeth, to the glowering darkness in Merrick's eyes. "What is wrong with you two?"

Helene turned to her, and with the most blatantly false expression Amy had ever seen on her mother's face, she said, "Why, nothing. Would you like some dessert, darling?"

"Dessert?" Amy knew she'd learned most of her people-pleasing ways from her mother, but offering dessert at this particular moment seemed the height of denial. "Mom...?"

"This is not working, Helene," Merrick said. "I think it's time we—"

"It's Annie's strawberry shortcake," Helene cut him off. "You know how lovely her shortcake is. The Green Market had a fresh crop of strawberries today and they are simply perfect. Now, who wants whipping cream?"

Amy sent an imploring glance her father's way, which he ignored, nodding instead. "Yes, of course," he said. "Whipping cream. By all means, don't leave off the whipping cream."

When Helene disappeared into the kitchen, Amy bent to scoop up the slivers of broken china and wondered if she dared ask her father what was going on. A part of her wanted to do exactly what Helene was doing, pretend that nothing out of the ordinary was happening.

The other part of her, which she'd also learned from her mother, called on her to find out what the problem was and fix it.

When she'd placed all the china chips in a tidy stack in her saucer, she looked at Merrick, who stared broodingly at the brandy decanter. Could her father be drinking too much? That seemed almost laughably unlikely.

But what was happening here tonight didn't feel at all laughable.

"Dad, what in the world is going on between you two?"

Merrick squirmed in his rocker and didn't look at her. "I think maybe you'd better ask your mother."

His evasiveness increased her level of distress. "You're not...Doc Yount hasn't said anything's... wrong, has he?"

"No, no," Merrick said. "I'm healthy as a horse. And so's your mother."

"Then what?"

He looked at her, his lips pursed grimly. She spotted the moment he made a decision, saw it flicker across his eyes. He leaned forward, about to speak, when Helene's voice floated to them, coming closer. "Here we are. Strawberry shortcake for everyone. Isn't this lovely?"

Amy couldn't have said whether it was lovely or not, she realized as she walked down the beach an hour later toward her own small cottage. Her memory of the entire evening was overshadowed by the specter of whatever was going wrong between her parents.

Her family already felt so fragmented. Amy knew she wouldn't be able to bear it if her parents' marriage was in trouble. She needed the stability she saw in their nearly fifty years together. Because it was all that remained of a family that had once felt so close, so warm, so connected. Tears stung the backs of Amy's eyes.

The disintegration had started with Lisa, years ago. One weekend Amy came home from Florida State University and found her younger sister completely changed. It was as if Lisa had vanished, leaving behind an empty body that was no longer willing to connect with anyone.

The emptiness that abandonment had created in Amy had been devastating. And no matter how she tried to find out what was wrong, to fix the problem, nothing had worked.

Megan's crisis had torn the final rent in the family.

Megan, two years older than Amy, married young, became a mother. But her husband was a navy SEAL and during one of his overseas tours, Megan and four-year-old Derek had come home to Hurricane Beach. Amy had loved the feeling of family that Megan and Derek had resurrected.

Until Derek disappeared. Vanished during a trip to the mall. The anguish of those awful days came back to Amy full force, even after all this time.

Because afterward, Megan, too, had disappeared. At first, her withdrawal, like Lisa's, had only been emotional. She'd stayed for a while, hoping beyond hope that Derek would come safely home. When hope finally died, she left Hurricane Beach. She left her marriage, her family and all reminders of a pain too great to bear.

In the dozen years since, only Amy and her parents retained the closeness that used to encompass all the Hardaways. Grace had filled some of the void left by Megan and Lisa. In fact, Amy needed a certain closeness to almost everyone in Hurricane

Beach, to ward off the feelings of isolation that came whenever she thought of the sisters she had lost.

And now something was wrong with Helene and Merrick.

By the time she spotted the warm lights of her cottage winking at her in the distance, Amy felt an urgent need to act, to do something to keep her fears from becoming reality. Maybe she could fix this before things became any more serious. She ran the last quarter mile to her beach house, her shoes squeaking in the sugar-fine sand. She dashed up the steps to the board walkway over the dunes, throwing open the door she forgot to lock half the time. Without pausing to catch her breath or greet the drowsy golden retriever, Sam, who peeked at her from his favorite spot on the couch, she grabbed the telephone and punched out Megan's Nebraska number.

"Be home," she whispered.

Sam responded with a whine and a yawn.

Her sister's reserved voice snapped Amy out of the anxiety that had almost overwhelmed her on the beach. What would she say now that she had Megan on the phone? The days for small talk between the three Hardaway sisters had long since disappeared.

"What is it, Amy?" Megan asked after a few awkward seconds. "Is something wrong?"

"Well, I..." Should she tell her sister? Would it serve any good purpose to worry her? Weighing her options, she stumbled along, breathless and unsure of her actions. "I've been thinking...that is, I think

Mom and Dad would really like to see us. All. Together. Maybe at Spring Break. Remember how much we used to love Spring Break?''

She heard the silence on the other end, louder even than the uneasy pounding of her heart.

"There's something wrong with one of them, isn't there? Amy, don't you dare keep it from me if one of them is sick."

"No, no, it isn't that. At least, I don't think so. They're just acting funny, that's all."

"Funny how?" Megan sounded impatient now.

"They were fighting."

"*Fighting?*"

"You know. Arguing."

"*Mom* and *Dad?*"

With some satisfaction, Amy heard the note of alarm come into her sister's voice. "I think you should come, Megan."

"I don't know. Maybe. I'm going to call Mom. Right now. You're sure you didn't imagine this?"

"I'm sure. Call me back, okay?"

"Maybe."

Amy sat on the arm of the couch after she hung up, waiting, worrying. But already feeling better because she wasn't in this alone. She had her sister now.

HELENE STOOD in the doorway that opened onto the deck. The hurricane lamps had been extinguished, and she could barely make out the dark outline of Merrick's shoulders.

Things hadn't gone at all the way she'd planned and she didn't know what to do about it.

She had tidied the kitchen and dressed for bed without hearing a peep out of her husband. Indeed, she hadn't felt inclined to speak to him, either, for a while. Her anger had stunned her; she couldn't remember the last time she'd been upset with Merrick, or he with her. And for a little while, she had whirled around the kitchen, drunk on indignation, clattering silverware and banging cabinet doors. Now, however, her pique had evaporated, leaving behind only regret. This little charade of theirs had been quite an unpleasant business, after all. Perhaps Merrick had been right.

"Are you coming to bed?" she asked softly, painfully aware that for the first time in their nearly fifty years together she was fearful of his response.

"You might have prepared me." His voice was gruff. "I didn't know part of the plan was to paint me as a drunkard."

"Oh, Merrick, I didn't plan it. It was...improvisation."

He didn't reply. The force of his displeasure struck her and the tears that had been lurking began to trickle down her cheeks. She turned to go in, unwilling for him to see that his distance hurt so much. The phone rang as she passed and she picked it up

without thinking. She realized as soon as she said
hello that her voice sounded funny. Teary.

*Oh, dear.*

AMY'S PHONE RANG five minutes later. She snatched
the receiver. Megan said, "She was crying."

"Crying?" Amy wailed.

"I want you to keep me posted."

"What did she say? Did she tell you anything?"

"Nothing. What were they fighting about?"

Amy struggled to remember. "Nothing. Little
stuff. Except..."

"Except what?"

"She seemed to think he was drinking too
much."

"Well, was he?"

"No. No more than usual. I don't know."

Megan sighed heavily. "I suppose if I really want
to know anything, I'm going to have to see for myself."

Amy's relief deepened. "Then you'll come? For
Spring Break."

Megan didn't commit, but Amy felt certain her
sister could be convinced now that she'd heard their
breezy, easygoing mother crying. Especially when
Megan said, "But who's going to convince Lisa to
show up?"

Amy drew a long, calming breath. The face of
Jon Costas came to mind. He was smiling. Not at
her, of course. But that didn't matter. The smile still

touched her, made her feel better. Even if it was for Lisa.

*Especially* because it was for Lisa, she amended. "I'll take care of Lisa."

JON LIKED closing the bakery. It was the only part of his new job he really liked. Everyone left, things were quiet, he was alone to deal with money and a ledger book—things he could handle.

He found himself stretching out the process of reconciling the register and preparing the deposit.

"Stalling," he muttered as he locked the back door. Walking down the alley and out onto Gulfview Lane, he noticed the sharp scent of saltwater wafting in on the heavy breeze off the gulf.

Unbidden, Amy popped into his head. He thought of the way her long hair curled and frizzed. It was a moment before he realized that he'd been thinking of Amy without a single intrusive thought of his failed marriage. That should have pleased him, but somehow it made him uneasy.

Jon dropped the money bag into the bank's night deposit, shoved his hands into his pockets and headed for home, sorry he didn't have a long subway ride ahead of him.

He was home in five minutes.

As he had come to expect, the family started in as soon as he walked through the front door. His father was standing at the bottom of the stairs, shouting in Greek and shaking his fist. A door slammed

upstairs. His mother came in from the kitchen, a
ladle in her hand, a clean apron over her navy dress.

"Thank goodness you are here," Leda said.
"You must tell this crazy man that he cannot treat
the child this way or—"

"No!" Demetri said, abandoning his Greek and
turning to face his wife and son. "For you I must
coddle and spoil her the way you did her father and
then she will end up like him, a drug fiend and a
bum. That will be better?"

Fighting the urge to turn and walk out, Jon
dropped his windbreaker onto a cast-iron hook on
the hall tree beside the door. The hardest part of this
whole business of moving back to Hurricane Beach
was not relearning the bakery business, but dealing
with his family. After being on his own for years—
ever since he and Lisa split—he felt overwhelmed,
suffocated by his family's demands. Every night, it
seemed, he came home to this quaint-looking Victorian house where he'd grown up, a house chock-
full of crocheted doilies and cabbage-rose wallpaper,
and walked smack into the middle of a grand, mel-
odramatic fight.

"What's wrong?" he asked, loudly enough to cut
through his parents' raised voices.

His mother gestured at his father, as if to say, he's
the one with the problem. Demetri launched into a
Greek diatribe that Jon had long since forgotten how
to interpret. Jon lifted both his hands and shook his
head.

"Mama, help me out here," he said. "What's Kieran done this time to set him off?"

Leda shrugged. "So she is a little computer-crazy. For this who can blame her, I ask you?"

Demetri grunted. "A little crazy? She stays in that room with her face stuck to this machine while her grandmother slaves all day over the stove—*three* stoves—then comes home to slave over another one. And this one—" he gestured up the stairs "—this one cannot be bothered to help."

"Probably she does homework," Leda began, and Jon realized that the argument would do nothing but continue in the same cycle until he intervened. Until he accepted the role they expected him to take—the reluctant substitute father.

"I'll talk to her," he said, and began climbing the stairs.

Demetri nodded approvingly. "You see. This girl needs a firm hand. You straighten her out, Jon."

Leda said, "Jon, you be gentle. After all..."

She didn't finish, but Jon knew what she was getting at. Kieran's mother had died five years ago, and her father had disappeared a month ago. If Jon said the wrong thing, the poor child would probably be warped for life.

Terrific.

His knock was met with silence, as he'd known it would be. This was not his first round with his niece. He knocked a second time and said, "I'm coming in."

The room was a study in neatness. Everything was in perfect order, except for the young girl herself. Kieran sat at her desk, keyboard in her lap, bare feet propped beside the color monitor of the high-end system Nick had bought his daughter for her last birthday.

Kieran ignored Jon, remaining entirely focused on the computer game playing out on her screen, a game of swords and cannons and shrieks from scantily clad but generously built women. Blood and guts and an occasional spurt of profanity.

Jon studied his niece, this teenager he barely knew, and wondered why he'd been chosen to become surrogate father. Surely his sister, Christa, who had three of her own, would be a better choice to finish raising this child.

But Christa had already told him that most people in Hurricane Beach didn't want Kieran associating with their children—and she didn't blame them. Kieran looked like trouble. Her dark eyes were defiant and mistrustful, if you could engage them at all. She was working on turning her lustrous black hair into dreadlocks. She dressed in torn jeans and T-shirts ripped off just below her budding breasts and she wore a tiny gold ring through her right nostril.

Kieran was bright and cute, but no one would ever guess it to look at her.

Jon acknowledged to himself that this was one of

Nick's little messes that he might not be able to straighten out before he returned to his real life.

Still, he had to try.

"Why don't you come down and help Grandma with dinner," he said, trying to speak over the booms and shrieks coming from her computer.

She ignored him, continued blasting away at her on-screen enemies.

Irritated, Jon strode across the room and pushed the power button on her hard drive. Her screen went black.

"Butthead."

The dispassion with which she addressed him gave Jon a chill. "Come help with dinner, Kieran. Your grandmother has worked all day. She's tired. Let's help her."

"I'm not hungry."

His niece frightened him. No wonder his mother backed down from confrontations with her.

"Come down with me anyway," he said softly. "Tell me about your day. I want to get to know you better."

She looked at him then, those dark eyes of hers filled with contempt. "Oh, puh-lease."

Jon felt his face grow warm. He was an unarmed man here and she knew it as well as he did. "Look, I know I'm not very good at this, so maybe you'll cut me some slack. Okay?"

"Bug off, why don't you?"

She jabbed at the power button. The computer

whirred to life again. Angry and humiliated, Jon thought seriously about yanking the computer right out of the wall and pitching it through her bedroom window. But his mother's plea came back to him. The wrong step on his part, and Kieran might be scarred for life.

*Right. Like she isn't already. Nick, you pathetic piece of...*

"You can't shut yourself up like this forever," he said, backing toward the door.

"Can't I?"

"I won't let you."

"You can't stop me," she said just before the electronic shrieks and booms started up again.

Jon feared she was right. With the tools he had at hand, he hadn't a prayer of stopping her.

AMY HAD to look up Lisa's number. She'd postponed calling her younger sister until tonight.

She pulled Sam into her lap—as much of the golden retriever as she could get into her lap, at any rate. "How's this?" she asked the dog. "Mom's been crying and Dad might be drinking too much and Megan and I want you to get right down here and save the day."

Sam gave her a baleful look, his solemn brown eyes seeming to infer that she must have been drinking too much, herself.

"Okay, Sam. Not a prayer. That's all you had to say. No need to get insulting." Amy twisted her tiny address book in her hands. "I've got it. We've all decided that what we want more than anything is one of those big, happy family celebrations like we used to have during Spring Break. Won't that be fun?"

Sam groaned and rolled onto his back. Amy rubbed his furry belly. "Well, I do have one more idea. This one's the best of all. I could call her up and say, 'Guess who's back in town and dying to see you?'"

With that, Sam scrambled off the couch and stared at her.

"You're wrong, Sam," she said. "And so is Grace. My plan *will* work."

She picked up the phone, spurred on by the memory of Jon Costas. He'd looked so good again this morning, rolling out pastry dough, those brown arms bare to the elbow. If Lisa saw him like that, how could she say no? What woman could?

Of course, something had gone wrong when they'd been married, Amy reminded herself.

Frowning, Amy dialed her sister's number in Connecticut, her heart pounding. She wouldn't mention Jon Costas. Jon would be her little surprise.

Despite the late hour, an answering machine kicked in. Almost relieved that she didn't have to talk to her sister, Amy left her number and hung up. It saddened her that even on tape Lisa's cool voice intimidated her.

But it wouldn't be that way for long. Lisa would

come back. With one look, Lisa and Jon would fall
head over heels again. Which, of course, meant Lisa
would have to come home for good.

Okay, okay. So Amy was working on a fairy tale.
She knew that. But she also knew that—with a little
human help—some fairy tales did come true. After
all, Jon and Lisa had been in love once. And it was
clear that neither one was happy right now.

Amy smiled at the prospect of having her sister
back, and ignored the twinge of doubt that it would
ever happen.

She also ignored her uneasiness at the prospect of
having to treat Jon Costas like a brother again. She'd
done it before and she could do it again. After all,
she was more mature now.

For her sister, she could do anything.

In fact, she would begin practicing right away.

# CHAPTER FOUR

AMY LET GO of the ladder on which her partner perched and dashed for the front window of their shop.

"Girl, if I die here because you can't sit still, my ghost will haunt you forevermore," Grace called out.

Amy glanced at Grace, who was pinning one of their newest arrivals—a metallic swimsuit and matching cover-up—to the wall above the swimsuit rack. Deciding her partner was in no immediate danger of falling, Amy peered between the summer rompers displayed in the front window.

Jon Costas had just walked into the bookstore next door. Amy's heart leaped.

"It's him!" She headed for the door. "I'll be right back. We need the morning paper, right?"

"We already have the morning paper! What I need is help getting off this ladder without breaking my neck."

"Okay! Okay!" Amy scurried back to her friend, placed one hand on the ladder and extended the other to Grace. "But hurry."

Grace didn't hurry. A few moments later, with

Amy still steadying the ladder, Jon went past the front window again, toward the bakery, his nose stuck in a copy of the *Wall Street Journal*. Amy sighed. It had been like this ever since the night she'd walked him home from the merchants' association meeting. Jon had managed to avoid her for days. He barely spoke when she came into the bakery every morning, no matter how chatty she was. And one night, when she'd locked up late and timed her departure for the bank's night drop to correspond with his, he'd suddenly remembered something he'd failed to do and went back to the bakery.

She'd offered to accompany him, but he'd forestalled her with a brisk, "No need."

Clearly, her ex-brother-in-law was giving her attempts at sisterly chumminess the brush-off.

"I'm beginning to think he and Lisa already know what I'm up to," she said to Grace, who had stepped down from the ladder and was studying the newly pinned-up bathing suit from across the small shop.

"It's lopsided," Grace said. "And I guess it'll stay that way until we hire that part-timer you keep saying is going to make our lives so much easier."

"I'll put a sign in the window today. We have to have someone by Spring Break."

Grace went to the back room and returned with soft drinks. "So Lisa hasn't called back?"

"No. I've left a message every night this week. I even called her business number once, and talked to her partner. But I'm beginning to think Lisa doesn't want to talk to me." She opened the soft-drink can and took a long swallow. "Either that or aliens have captured her and won't let her call in for messages."

"Give it up, Amy. Nobody appointed you to fix everybody's life, you know."

"That shows how little you know. Check my wallet and you'll find my licence to fix anything that's not working, right next to my library card."

Their good-natured bickering stopped only long enough for Amy to help the customer who came in looking for a cocktail dress to wear to a reunion in Tallahassee. Then came two teenagers who giggled over the prices and tried on dozens of items before going out empty-handed.

After the customers left, Amy balled up a T-shirt that now had a ring of makeup on the collar and pitched it at her partner. "Besides," she said, resuming their earlier conversation, "it's not like I'm interfering with strangers. This is Mom and Dad I'm talking about."

"Everybody has a tiff from time to time, Amy. It's not the end of the world."

"But they're acting so weird."

"That's a family trait, isn't it?"

"Not funny, Grace. You should have seen Mom when I ran into her at the Green Market the other day. She was fluttering. The way she does when she's upset. You know, her hands, her lips, even her eyelashes. Like a trapped bird who won't give up the search for the way out. All she would say was that it would blow over.''

"So? What's wrong with that?''

"She won't tell me *what* will blow over. And neither will Dad.''

"You hounding him, too?''

"I ran into him on the beach. He was walking. *Alone*.'' Everyone in Hurricane Beach knew that Merrick and Helene walked together every afternoon. "He said I should let them work it out.''

"Listen to your father, girl.''

Amy dropped into the chair beside the dressing room. "It's just...they've never shut me out before.''

Her sisters, yes. But never her parents.

Grace dropped to her knees and put an arm around Amy's shoulders. "Maybe this is all for the best. You know, a little venting. Imagine that you had to keep your mouth shut even for fifty minutes, much less fifty years. Think how nuts you'd be.''

"I could do it.''

"Ha! Not even fifty seconds.''

Amy scowled at Grace. But she didn't challenge her.

She had no intention, however, of giving up on either of her projects. In fact, she simply redoubled her efforts to find the perfect way to worm her way into her ex-brother-in-law's life. She talked to his uncle Nikos, who told her that everyone in the family was concerned that Jon wasn't getting out much since his return home.

"But the women, they are working on that," Nikos said.

"What do you mean?"

Nikos shook his head. "They look for a wife. That's the answer, they say. Find the boy a wife. And no more mistakes. This time, a *Greek* wife."

The discovery that the Costas clan was engaged in a little matchmaking made it all the more urgent that Amy get her plan off the ground as quickly as possible.

Aurelia was the only one who gave Amy any real help in figuring out how to get close to Jon. The older woman revealed that Jon disappeared for a couple of hours every afternoon. She looked over her shoulder and whispered, "And I know where he goes. Every day. Three sharp. You could time your baklava by it."

"Where?"

"To the beach. To jog." She rolled her eyes and fanned her face with the back of her hand. "He puts on the shoes, he puts on the shorts, he goes, he runs. He comes back sweaty. I say, is this any way to make our customers want to shop here?" She shrugged. "He just grins. That boy, when he grins, how you gonna say no to him, that's what I want to know. How you gonna say no?"

"I don't see how anyone could," Amy agreed solemnly.

That afternoon, when she went to Rêve Rags, she went straight to the back of the shop. "We got any running shoes in stock?" she called out front to her partner.

Grace got up from the computer, where she was updating the inventory, and joined Amy in the back. "Running shoes? I thought you were allergic to exercise."

She picked up a pair and checked the size. "Grace, I'm not getting any younger. Don't you think it's time I whipped myself into shape?"

MERRICK HARDAWAY watched his wife's face as the man from Atlanta described his development company's vision of Hurricane Beach. He knew before Palmer Boyce ever finished speaking exactly how Helene would react.

That's what fifty years of intimacy—come the end of the summer—bought, he supposed. The ability to tune in to little things like the way she twisted an earring when she didn't like what she was hearing. Helene was the flip side of his soul.

*Then why the hell haven't we exchanged a civil word for weeks?* he wondered irritably.

She glanced at him, no doubt caught him frowning at her again and looked away, worry in her sea-green eyes. *Dammit all.*

Palmer Boyce was winding down, honoring them both with the self-satisfied smile of a man who knew money talked and assumed the amount of money he'd tossed out would speak loud and clear. "Are there any questions at this point?"

Helene looked overwhelmed. Merrick had plenty of questions, but he wasn't in the mood to discuss them now. He stood. "Not for the moment. But thank you so much for coming and we'll be in touch if we need more information."

Palmer Boyce was out the front door in minutes.

"Well, I'm certainly glad you got rid of him," Helene said, scooping up the colorful brochures Palmer Boyce had left. "What an abysmal idea that was."

"From one point of view, yes." Merrick watched his wife toss the literature into the wastebasket and knew he was about to wade into turbulent seas. "From another, perhaps an idea worthy of consideration."

Helene faced him. "Selling Sea Haven so those vultures can build condos and hotels and golf courses? I can't imagine a more awful plan."

"Perhaps it's time Hurricane Beach experienced a little growth. A little prosperity."

"Hurricane Beach has all the prosperity it needs. And so do we," Helene said adamantly. "You can't be serious."

Merrick knew, of course, that the majority of people who lived, worked, owned property in Hurricane Beach would agree with his wife's outrage. Zoning laws and other regulations had been carefully structured over the years to protect this tiny oasis of calm in the midst of the booming development that had swallowed virtually every mile of Florida beach. Most of the people in Hurricane Beach, even the small-business owners like his daughter, made a comfortable living and enjoyed the low-key existence Hurricane Beach offered.

But it wasn't the visions of golf carts and eight-story condos that appealed to Merrick. It wasn't even the eight-figure sum that Palmer Boyce had mentioned, a figure Merrick strongly suspected was only a starting point.

"I am serious," he said. "I'm looking at this from the standpoint of a father."

"A father?" Helene sank back into the over-stuffed chair across from him. "What on earth do you mean by that?"

"Only that you continue to fret that our girls aren't close. And it occurred to me, as I listened to our man Boyce, that leaving them a parcel of valuable property might only lead to more dissension."

"Merrick, Sea Haven is their birthright. You know that. We couldn't possibly sell it out from under them."

"Suppose one of them wants to sell? Suppose they can't agree on what to do with the property. What kind of birthright is it if their inheritance is the blow that drives them apart for good?"

Helene shook her head, and the twisting of the earring began.

"Think of it, my love. No bickering. No jealousy. No more reason for animosity."

Helene stood up abruptly. "And no more reason to ever lay eyes on one another. I can't believe you're even suggesting this. I feel as if...as if...I don't even know you anymore!"

BY MIDAFTERNOON, when the day's baking was done and most of Hurricane Beach had finished its daily shopping, Jon liked to get away. He usually started by waiting on the pier to watch his cousin Jimmy's boats come in. He always enjoyed the spectacle of the boats returning with their catch. From a distance, the boats looked glamorous, graceful, their white hulls shining against the water, the brown, shirtless bodies of their crews laboring effortlessly. But Jon liked the moment when the boats drew so close they became real, when he could tell the paint was chipped and the engines chugged and the activity onboard looked frenzied instead of choreographed.

He waved and tried not to feel envy when the boats made their lumbering turn into Alligator Bay. Even at a distance, he got whiffs of the ripe smell of shrimp and grouper and sea air, the equally ripe sounds of the profanity being tossed back and forth between his host of cousins and nephews. He remembered the rough feel of net in his hands and the way the sun baked his skin.

He felt restless and eager.

Today, as he always did, Jimmy waved and called to him, "Hey, Mr. Moneybags!"

Jon couldn't hear his cousin for the sound of the boats, but he knew what Jimmy said. His cousin's good-natured ribbing hadn't changed much over the years.

When the boats disappeared behind the marina, Jon set out down the beach for his daily jog. After a mile or two, he was aware of nothing but the wind whipping his hair, the haunting call of the gulls and the steady roar of the surf marking the pace as his shoes hit the sand.

By the time an hour had passed, he had almost lulled himself to the point where he was ready to go back, close up shop for the day and face whatever waited at home.

But something about the figure ahead on the beach struck a chord. The long legs, pulled tightly against the chest and held there by long arms, were delicately pale. But the dead giveaway was the mass of strawberry-blond hair wrapped in a tangled cross between a ponytail and a bun.

Amy.

The split second of recognition brought back a memory Jon had all but forgotten.

He'd been in Miami several years, going to school off and on, mostly just glad to be far enough away to avoid his grasping, clutching family. They'd wailed long and hard when he'd gone, leaving behind the would-be fiancée they had selected for him.

Jon liked the freedom in Miami. He went to classes when he wanted to and worked at what he wanted to.

He'd been about to enroll for his second term of work on his MBA when he looked up in the campus library one day and saw her sitting across the room, curled in a chair, biting down on a pencil and frowning over a textbook.

For that first second, he'd thought she was Amy Hardaway and his heart had leaped. He was on his feet and across the room, a smile on his lips, when he realized it wasn't Amy. It was her younger sister, Lisa.

That was how it had started.

Jon shook his head to clear it and thought about turning around, finishing his run in the opposite direction. But before he could act on the thought, Amy turned her face in his direction and raised a long, sleek arm to wave at him.

Caught.

He faltered, trapped between wanting to get away and knowing it would be pointless to try. Amy Hardaway was nothing if not relentless. She *had* warned him, after all.

She fell into place beside him, smiling. "Hi. Mind if I join you?"

He had to admit that part of him wanted her company. But the question was moot. Amy had already launched into one of her monologues as she ran.

"So I decided it was time to get in better shape," she finished, a little breathless.

She looked in terrific shape to him already, but he refrained from saying so. He wanted to refrain from thinking so.

"How far do you run?" she asked him.

"Four or five miles."

She groaned. "I'll never keep up for that long."

He realized he had slowed his pace to make it easier for her.

Jon wanted to be nice to her. He really did. Unfortunately, Amy—his ex-sister-in-law, he reminded himself—had become yet another source of frustration for him. He thought about her too much. Way too much. In ways that a guy just didn't think about a woman who was family. Practically family. Used to be family. Any normal man, that would have been no problem. Because any normal man would have understood that an ex-sister-in-law was off-limits and simply accept the friendship she offered, no strings attached.

Jon couldn't seem to grasp that.

"You come out every afternoon?" she asked.

And he knew that the wrong response would rob him of his one pleasure in Hurricane Beach.

"No, I, ah…" Lying gave him a sour feeling in his gut. "What about the shop? Shouldn't you be at the shop?"

"Well, I'm supposed to be running off copies of flyers—we're looking for part-time help. But Wayne

had closed up the copy shop for an hour—I think
he had to take his car to the garage for new brakes—
so, here I am. Killing time.''

He nodded. How could he be nice to her and dis-
courage her at the same time?

"Are things settling down for you?'' she asked.

"Settling down. Sure,'' he said, and the little
white lie gnawed at him again. "Well, maybe not.''

"Family making you crazy?''

He wondered how she knew, then realized she
knew his family pretty well. He'd seen how they
'treated her, like one of the Costas girls. He grinned.
"How'd you guess?''

"It might be the way your jaw works every time
your *thea* Aurelia tells you to punch that dough
down one more time.'' She switched into an imita-
tion of his aunt's voice. "'This time like you mean
business. Yes?'''

He laughed at the perfect image her impersona-
tion conjured. And he made the mistake of looking
at her when he did so. His laughter died in his throat.
He liked the sight of her dimpled smile. He liked
the liberal dusting of freckles across her nose, and
the way they drifted into sparseness on her cheeks.
Strands of golden-red hair were already floating free
from the ponytail, trailing down her back, except
where the sea breeze lifted them.

Even in the unflinching glare of midmorning sunshine, she was perfection. He looked away before
she could see the admiration in his eyes.

"You have to learn to play duck." Her gossamer voice urged him to look her way again.

"Play duck?"

"You ever watch a duck go underwater, then come back to the surface? The way the water rolls off its back? That's what you have to do. Learn to let it all roll off your back."

He thought of Kieran. "Easy to say."

"You know, I can't do all the talking myself," she said, her breathy voice more breathless than usual.

"Nothing wrong with silence."

Apparently, Amy didn't concur. "You never were very talkative. Even in school, all those years ago."

He was surprised she remembered him from that long ago, but he didn't say so. "You weren't either."

She laughed. "I know. I was tongue-tied. Around... everybody. I can't believe you'd even remember that."

It felt strange, hearing her echo his own insecurities. He thought of coming clean, telling her about the crush he'd nursed all those years ago. But he didn't think that was a smart path to go down. Nothing he thought around Amy seemed safe to say aloud.

"Twenty years," he said instead. "Hard to believe."

"Not for me," she said. "Don't you feel different? As if all that happened to somebody else? In another lifetime?"

"Is that how you feel?"

She nodded. "Like those were the cocoon years. I was all wrapped up, stuck in the dark. The only thing I had going for me was two great sisters—they made up for the rest of it."

"The rest of what? Seems to me you Hardaway girls had it knocked. You were rich and good-looking and smart. What else did you need?"

She stared at him as if he'd suddenly begun speaking Greek. "Were you in the same Hurricane Beach I was in?"

"No, as a matter of fact. My parents were immigrants, and poor working stiffs, besides. My grades were in the toilet most of the time."

"But your family is so close. How bad could things be if your family is close?"

"How bad? How about a family so close they want to pick your girlfriends. A family so close you not only live in the same house with them, you have to work in the same business with them. A family so close you don't even get to eat what the other kids eat. You got burgers and pizza, we had gyros and souvlaki."

"Oh."

Her bewildered expression made him want to soften the picture he'd created. "Other than that, though, it wasn't so bad."

She laughed then and he felt better.

"Those things pale compared to my adolescent traumas," she said. "Like being taller than any boy in the ninth grade and a beanpole, besides. Overbite. I still have overbite."

She demonstrated for him, and he laughed at the face she made while baring her even white teeth.

"Braces can only do so much," she said.

"I don't remember you wearing braces."

"See. I knew you didn't remember me. You're probably thinking of Megan. Now, Megan was always beautiful. Or Lisa. Did you have a thing for Lisa all along? I'll bet you did, didn't you?"

"No," he said, and tried to keep from sounding too sharp.

"Did I tell you about her house in Danfield, Connecticut?"

Jon let her ramble on, barely listening to what she said. He told himself he could tune her out, listen to the beach sounds. But he realized what he was tuning in to was the soft melody of Amy's voice. He didn't give a damn what she was talking about, the sound of her was enough.

When he finished his run, he told himself he hadn't encouraged her. But encouragement apparently wasn't necessary. Amy turned up the next day and the next. On the third day, a big lumbering dog she called Sam joined them and Jon grew even more squeamish over the image of them running along the beach, one big happy family. Man, woman, dog. The perfect picture. He began looking over his shoulder, worried someone in the Costas family would see them and make something of the time he was spending with his ex-sister-in-law.

But no one saw them, and the only one who seemed inclined to make something of it was him.

"Why no man in your life?" he asked one day, thinking if he asked all the questions himself he wouldn't have to fight so hard to keep from saying the wrong thing.

"Oh." The question seemed to startle her, as if it hadn't occurred to her before. "Well. I don't know. I suppose because it's a small town and most guys my age are already taken."

He tried to think of eligible men around their age and had to admit there were few in Hurricane Beach. And he wasn't inclined to point out the few who came to mind. Could that be construed as jealousy? he wondered. "Then why don't you leave?"

"Leave? Hurricane Beach is home. I have family here. Mom and Dad. And Grace. She's practically family now. Really, the whole town is kind of like family. Don't you feel that? Even being gone so long?"

"The last thing I need is more family."

"So that's why you left in the first place? To get away from family?"

"Partly. Yeah. I suppose so."

"And Lisa? Is that why Lisa left?"

He heard wistfulness in her voice and looked at

her. Her perpetual smile had disappeared. For once, Jon didn't feel the urge to be evasive with her.

"I honestly don't know why Lisa left."

Understanding, and a kind of resignation, swept across Amy's face. He knew exactly what it signified. Apparently, he wasn't the only one Lisa kept at arm's length. He remembered how close the three Hardaway sisters had seemed when they were kids, and wondered if whatever had driven the wedge between them was the same thing that had made it so damn hard for him to get close to Lisa.

Or was it just him? After all, look at the way he was acting with Amy. Shutting her out. Fending off her attempts to be friendly. Who could stay married to a man like that?

"I guess I'm not very good at the intimacy thing," he said, wanting to give Amy something to ease the forlorn look in her soft green eyes. "Not then. Not now."

"It takes time," she said. "People change. Why, I bet you'll be surprised how much Lisa has changed when you see her during Spring Break."

"Lisa's coming back?"

"Well, we haven't pinned down all the details. But I'm certain she'll be here. You know, it would probably be nice if the two of you had dinner one night. You know, to smooth off the rough edges. Show there's no hard feelings, that kind of thing. Don't you think that would be nice?"

Jon wanted to tell her there was no need, that no

hard feelings lingered between him and Lisa. It was true on his part, at least, and he hoped Lisa felt the same. Whatever had drawn him and Lisa together all those years ago had died quickly, once each of them had realized that the other didn't hold the key to wholeness.

He wanted to tell Amy those things, but he didn't. Because he felt safer having her think he still carried some kind of torch for her sister.

Then maybe she wouldn't notice how her presence affected him. Maybe no one would notice. And maybe, after a while, he could even stop noticing it himself.

# CHAPTER FIVE

AMY STASHED the small canvas bag of change under her arm and turned away from the bank counter. Across the lobby, giving away a million-dollar smile to the dour-faced bank manager, was Jon.

She stood still for a few moments, pleased to contemplate how well her plan was working. How close—how much like brother and sister—she and Jon had grown the last week. Then when voices drifted to her from the nearby cubicles where people accessed their safe-deposit boxes.

The voices were familiar. So was the tone—tense and angry.

"This was your idea, but I don't have to like it," Helene Merrick was saying.

"It can't hurt to have the property appraised, Helene. Then, if we decide this is the right thing to do, it will be a simple matter."

"This will never be a simple matter."

"All I mean is, it will give us an idea how much there'll be to divide up."

"Whatever you say, Merrick."

The two voices from the cubicle grew quiet. Unable to risk facing her parents, Amy walked out of the bank in a daze. Appraisals? Dividing property? Her parents could have been discussing only one thing.

Divorce.

An ache wrapped itself tightly around Amy's heart. Her parents, divorcing?

Whatever she had to do, she couldn't let that happen.

SLAPPING HIS NIECE'S report card against his thigh, Jon marched upstairs to Kieran's room and acted out the silly ritual of knocking while she ignored him.

Nothing was turning out right in Hurricane Beach. His parents staunchly refused to be convinced that he couldn't stay forever. His ex-sister-in-law continued her relentless pursuit, although it occurred to him she might leave him alone if he told her what her efforts were accomplishing. For he knew what she had in mind—some kind of grand scheme to bring him and Lisa back together.

What would she think, he wondered, if he told her that the only thing she had accomplished was to convince him that he might have picked the wrong Hardaway sister.

As if he needed another problem in his life, he thought as he entered his niece's room. Once again, the room was spotless and Kieran herself was a disaster area glued to her computer.

"We have to reach an understanding, Kieran," he said, sitting on the corner of her bed.

"The concerned-adult routine?" the teenager said. "You must've seen the report card."

He looked down at the marginal grades, noting the downward spiral they'd been on since the early part of the school year. "You want to talk about what's happening?"

"No."

He'd been prepared for that. "That's fine. I'll talk. You listen."

She stopped pecking on her keyboard, but she kept her eyes trained on the monitor.

"When I was your age, all of us—all the kids in the family—worked part-time at the bakery," he said, watching her back stiffen as his words registered. "We worked summers and we worked after school. You're fifteen. You can start next week."

"In your dreams."

Aware of a growing anger he didn't want to feel, Jon stood and walked around to face her. He took the keyboard out of her lap, placed it on the desk and looked down at her. She didn't budge. Jon realized his heart was racing. How do you bluff a teen into doing what you want her to? It sank in for the first time that the stakes here were a lot higher than they'd been on Wall Street, when the only thing he'd run the risk of losing was a few million dollars.

What if he lost Kieran?

His gut clenched at the thought. He wasn't very good at showing it, but Jon loved his niece. When she'd been little it had been easier to let her know how he felt. Now he didn't know how to show this troubled kid that the old feelings were still there. He knew there was a lot at stake. He'd seen kids like Kieran on the streets of New York City. Caring this much was suddenly very, very scary. For the first time in his life, he caught a glimpse of the emotions that had prompted his parents' frustrating attempts to control his life.

"Look at me or I'll turn off your computer again."

She rolled her eyes. Then looked at him. Jon tried not to let his relief show.

"I want you at the bakery starting Monday after school. I want you working this summer, too. And I want you helping your aunt Christa with her kids."

She made a bleat of protest.

"I know. I hated it, too." Hell, he pretty much hated it now, but he wasn't going to tell her that. "But it didn't exactly scar me for life. And maybe by the time school starts again in the fall, you'll have your head on straight."

He could almost see another wiseacre remark forming in her head, so he reached over, placed the keyboard back in her lap and said, "One hour a day on this thing or I cancel the service."

"You can't do that!"

"The hell I can't."

"My dad gave me this. And the on-line service."

"Well, your dad's not here right now. I am. So you answer to me now. Got it?"

He didn't wait for her answer. He closed her bedroom door behind him, stood in the hallway for a moment, eyes closed, willing his heartbeat to slow. When he opened his eyes, his mother stood on the next step from the top, looking at him with dismay and guilt in her expression. And for the first time, he understood precisely why she let her granddaughter get away with so much. She blamed herself for her son, for Nick's being a lousy father.

"Mama, it'll be okay," he said with more conviction than he felt. "She needs a firm hand."

He wondered where she would get that firm hand once he was gone. But he couldn't worry about that today.

KIERAN TYPED furiously for the next five minutes, fighting the urge to fling her computer against the wall, to destroy everything in this room she now considered her prison.

She hated them. Uncle Jon especially. He looked so much like her dad, sometimes it was all she could do to look at him without losing it.

How desperately happy she'd been when her grandmother had said her *theo* Jon was coming to stay, to take care of her. She'd always worshiped him, her glamorous, faraway uncle. And he was coming all this way just for her. Then she'd heard him, right after he arrived, talking to his sister, Christa.

"I don't know how to make it any more clear that

this is only temporary," he'd said. "I'm staying just long enough to get the store back on an even keel. I've told them, six months is about my limit. But they just don't listen."

Kieran's heart had shut him out then, refusing to allow him any closer. Because he would leave, too, the way her father had, the way her mother had. And she refused to be hurt by that again.

*Damn them all,* she thought as she pounded the keys that would ship her message into the right electronic mailbox.

She waited impatiently, cruising, making snide replies to postings on the "Star Trek" bulletin board, then sailing on to Adult Topics. Adults, she was discovering, sounded as juvenile when they hit the Net as high school boys hanging out at their lockers. Everything was a dirty joke.

Except for Hardball.

She checked her electronic mailbox. Every five minutes for the next hour, she checked for Hardball's reply. She grew more agitated with each passing minute. She had to talk to him, had to hear from somebody who understood her. By the time her grandmother called her for dinner, she still hadn't heard from him. She waited one more minute and checked again.

*Yes!*

Chill, Beach Bunny. You're not a kid. The old dude doesn't own you. Your path is your own.

Here's how you can show him just that.

Relief filled her as she read Hardball's reply. He always came through.

AMY JOGGED with Jon the next day and the next and the next. On the fourth day, she discovered that Jon wasn't waiting in his usual spot at the end of the pier. He was walking toward the docks.

Undaunted by the possibility that he'd changed his routine to avoid her, she followed him and reached the dock in time to overhear the end of his conversation with Jimmy.

"Good day?" Jon asked as Jimmy landed beside him on the narrow wooden pier that jutted out between the slips.

"Better than some," Jimmy answered. "Say, how about you join me and Alexis tonight at the Barnacle? We'll put on a feast. Whaddaya say?"

"Better make it another time," Jon said.

*At least,* Amy thought, *she wasn't the only one he was turning down.*

"Okay, but I mean for us to do it." Jimmy shook a finger at his cousin. "No weaseling out. And, say, I been thinking, you ought to meet Alexis's cousin from Miami. A nice Greek girl, and right up your alley, Mr. Moneybags."

Amy's heart lurched. Everyone was in on the plan to marry Jon off. This time to the right kind of girl, one who would fit in with his family. She should have realized it would be that way. She pasted on a big smile and collared Jon for their afternoon jog.

Still, her smile must not have fooled him. Before they'd been gone a half hour, he said, "Something's wrong."

Suddenly, she realized how desperately she longed to share with someone her fears about her parents. Through a restless night she had agonized over the prospect of a divorce. She had to talk to someone, but who? She glanced at Jon.

"You're so quiet," he said. "I figured something must be wrong."

"It's just...how do you handle it when you're worried about your family?"

He smiled wryly. "Ignore it and hope it'll go away?"

"No, you don't. If you did that, you wouldn't be here now."

"I'll give you a serious answer another time. For now, tell me what's bothering you."

He stopped and she slowed and turned back to him. For once, his dark eyes weren't inscrutable. She could read genuine concern there and it was all she needed to tell him about the dissension between her parents.

"I'm sure my parents still love each other," she said. "But what if they get a divorce and one of them goes away? Dad could go back to England, you know. I know they'd both regret it. And I will have lost another member of my family."

He put his arm around her and said, "Well, for now, nobody's divorcing anybody. Nobody's leaving you today."

"Yes, but—"

"And if anything like that happens, I promise to loan you my pop and mama, all my aunts and uncles, every cousin I possess."

The way he said it made her smile, made the fears seem less overwhelming for a moment.

That night, she'd thought about the gentleness in his voice and she'd slept better, even though nothing had changed.

By the fifth day, Amy was limping and hoping Jon wouldn't notice.

*Why are you doing this?* she asked herself, and she wasn't entirely sure she liked the answer. Persistence was one thing, but this business of throwing herself in Jon Costas's path had gone way beyond persistence.

And the worst of it was, she thought as she tried keeping up with him on the sand, the whole plan was beginning to feel as if it had backfired.

"What's wrong with your leg?" he asked.

"Nothing." Surely the tightness would go away soon. "Tell me what living in New York City was like," she said, trying to change the subject.

He glanced down at her leg, frowning. "You can't run through it, you know. It'll just get worse."

She was beginning to believe he was right. The muscle in her calf kept getting tighter and tighter.

Kind of like the wound-up feeling inside her whenever she was around Jon Costas. Emotions that had nothing to do with Lisa.

Actually, they had a lot to do with Lisa. Unless she could find some innocent explanation for her very un-sister-in-law-like reactions to Jon, she ran the risk of alienating her sister for good.

Nervous, she did what she always did. She launched into nosy, mindless conversation. To fill the silence.

"So, did you go to shows and galleries every week? Did you have a penthouse with a view of Central Park? Did you hate the traffic and the noise and the dirt, or did you think New York City was the most glorious place in the world?"

He looked at her and shook his head. Perspiration beaded in his silvery temples, streaked the sides of his face. He looked so male. So solid. She decided a man like Jon Costas could make any problem less frightening.

"I was a typical New Yorker," he said. "After my first year in the city, I never went to another Broadway show. I had a studio apartment overlooking an alleyful of Dumpsters. And I grumbled about everything. But only to other New Yorkers."

She laughed. Being around Jon was so easy, so much fun. Except when she noticed the dark hair on his arms and at his throat. Except when she followed the rise and fall of his chest and discovered it made her own breathing more shallow, and more rapid.

*That's the running,* she told herself. *Nothing but the running.*

"So when exactly is Lisa coming?" he said.

"Lisa?" Fine. *Now* he asks about Lisa. Now, when the very idea of him with her sister created this wellspring of...of... Needing at all costs to avoid thinking of it as jealousy, she said, "You've decided I'm right, then? About getting together with her."

"I didn't say that." And he looked at her, capturing her gaze with those deep brown eyes. "I just wondered how long before she showed up and caught us together."

"Caught us?"

He'd startled her, throwing her off-stride. Just as she realized from the gleam in his eyes that he was only teasing, she also realized she had come down too heavily on the leg that was already giving her trouble. Her calf muscle pulled. She cried out and automatically went down on one knee.

"I told you so," he said, taking her by the shoulders and easing her onto the sand.

"Well, that's certainly helpful," she grumbled, clutching her bunched-up calf muscle.

"Here," he said. "Let me."

"I can do it," she snapped, wanting to shoo away the long, lithe hands that had taken over her calf muscle. She tensed at the reaction that sizzled through her at his touch.

"Loosen up," he said.

Impossible. She leaned back on her hands, but discovered that watching him only made it worse. His skin was so dark beside hers, his arms and back and legs so densely muscled. She remembered the first time he'd rescued her, all the way back in junior high. She'd thought the feelings she'd had then were powerful. They were nothing compared to today's heart-stopping reaction.

She bent her neck and stared up at the sky, but the image of him stayed with her. As did the feel of his strong fingers working the muscle in her leg.

"See?" he said. "It's unclenching."

Irritated with herself, Amy said, "What a lucky woman I am. Stuck on a deserted beach with a sports injury and a bread-kneader."

He took her foot in one hand, held her calf in the other and began to flex her ankle, slowly, gently stretching out the strained calf muscle. "That's right. I'm a trained technician. Lucky for you I didn't start out grinding cinnamon."

Despite her discomfort, which was no longer located in her leg, but had meandered to a lot of other locations throughout her traitorous body, Amy laughed. "I'd be in a fine fix then, wouldn't I?"

He dropped to his seat, still flexing her ankle, and smiled into her eyes.

His smile disconcerted her all over again. "It's better, thank you."

"We don't want it tightening up again."

"I'm sure I can walk now." But she couldn't run,

which was what she wanted to do. Run in the opposite direction. Away from the warm feel of his skin on hers, the tender strength of his touch and the soft fire in his eyes.

"Give it a few more minutes," he said.

His voice seemed to urge her to something more intimate—to touch him back, perhaps. Once again, her imagination.

"No," she said, beginning to push herself to her feet. "It's really okay."

"If you aren't careful, I'll end up carrying you home."

She dropped back to the sand, imagined him sweeping her up in those strong, hard arms and cradling her against his chest all the way home. No, that would never do. "Okay. But you should finish your run. I'll be fine."

"I'm not going to leave you here by yourself."

She wished he would. His presence was too potent, too dangerous, and held a lot more peril than sitting here alone with a charley horse. Because what he stirred in her put too much at risk.

All she had to do was act on this strange, adolescent attraction to Jon and she would forever ruin any chance she had of mending her relationship with Lisa. And no man was worth losing her sister for good.

As the rest of her family crumbled around her, Amy knew that with certainty.

She would make everything right again, she vowed. And denying these feelings for Jon Costas was a small price to pay.

# CHAPTER SIX

AMY WAS LOSING her grip on everything.

She couldn't decide what to do about her parents; things were getting worse. Maida told her that one of her customers at the gallery had seen Helene walk out on Merrick during dinner at the Barnacle earlier in the week. Amy had tried talking to Bea Connell, who probably knew Helene better than anyone outside the family, but Bea had repeated the words Amy was growing weary of in a hurry: *Mind your own business, Amy.*

Nobody understood. She had to do something, before it was too late.

Then there was Jon and Lisa. Just this afternoon, Aurelia told her the Stephanopolis family was coming soon for a visit.

"Two marriageable daughters, the Stephanopolis family," Aurelia said with great satisfaction. "One a teacher, one a degree in home economics. Very good prospects."

Amy had to do something about Jon and Lisa before it was too late.

The plan came to her out of the blue one afternoon when Sam knocked her into the sand, planted his big paws on her chest and looked down at her with his expectant expression.

Ten minutes later, she was on the phone to Megan.

"Guess what? We're going to have a fiftieth wedding anniversary celebration for Mom and Dad. We'll get things rolling during Spring Break."

"An anniversary celebration? Amy, are you sure—"

"Of course I'm sure. How can they talk about divorce if the whole town's getting ready to celebrate their anniversary?"

"Divorce? They're talking about *divorce?*"

For an instant, Amy felt unsure. They had used the word, hadn't they? She couldn't remember precisely, but the implication was more than clear. "They were talking about property settlement. If that's not about divorce, I don't know what is."

"Oh dear." For once, Megan's calm reserve vanished. "Amy, if they're talking about getting a divorce, they may not be too crazy about the idea of a big party."

"Megan, they'll do anything to get the three of us together, won't they?"

"Well, yes."

"Then if they know you and Lisa are coming home for Spring Break to plan a big party, they wouldn't want to disappoint us, would they?"

"Well..."

"And if they just hang in there, whatever this is

that's coming between them, they'll surely get over
it by the end of the summer. Don't you think?''

"Well…"

"Of course they will. You just make your travel
plans. I'll take care of the rest.''

By the time they hung up, the plan was already
falling into place in Amy's mind. The celebration,
the nostalgia, the reunion with their three daughters,
all of it would serve to remind Helene and Merrick
how wonderful their fifty years together had been.
Their problems, whatever they might be, would
seem petty to them beside all that.

Amy felt satisfied just thinking about it.

"And the icing on the cake," she said as she
passed Sam a slice of cold leftover pizza from the
fridge, and munched on the other slice herself, "is
that Lisa will have to come home, too. And you
know what that means. Who knows, maybe we'll
even have wedding bells at the same time.''

Sam moaned.

"I know she hasn't called back," Amy said. "I'll
write her. That would probably be better, anyway. I
promise you, this is a great idea and it's going to
work perfectly.''

Sam quit wagging his tail, stared at her long and
hard, then retired to the couch for the evening.

"You're wrong," Amy retorted. "He's just a
friend. A brother.''

But as she joined Sam on the couch, envisioning
her inevitable success, the idea of Jon and Lisa join-

ing hands at the altar didn't give her the same thrill
it had when she'd first thought of the idea a few
weeks ago.

THE YOUNG GIRL wearing a ring in her nose and a
pair of jeans that were ready for the ragbag circled
the interior of the shop twice before Amy recognized
her as Kieran Costas, Jon's niece.

Amy approached the girl cautiously. "Looking
for something special?"

Kieran touched the shoulder of a chic black linen
column dress as if it carried a deadly virus and gave
Amy an incredulous look. "No."

"I'm Amy. If I can help you with anything, let
me know."

She turned back to the sales records she'd been
sorting. From the corner of her eye, she watched as
the teen shuffled around the store. Something
clutched inside her. She had the odd sensation that
she'd been in this girl's skin, knew exactly how she
felt. It occurred to her that, no matter how different
Kieran Costas looked on the outside, she must feel
a lot of the same things Amy Hardaway had felt at
that age. Misunderstood. Gawky and awkward and
unsure of herself, even as she was certain that everyone else faced life with supreme confidence.

To top it off, Kieran no doubt felt abandoned.

And Amy knew how much that hurt. If there was
anything she could do to help the teenager, Amy
decided she would try.

Kieran sidled closer, peered at Amy, then away. "You have a computer."

*Bingo!* Amy didn't look up, hoped her face didn't reveal the silent cheer her heart had sent up. "Yeah. We keep all our records on it. You know, who brings in what and on what date, what the price is, that kind of thing."

Kieran nodded, leaned over the handmade jewelry in the case.

"Problem is," Amy said, taking a calculated shot in the dark, "neither one of us is very up on computers."

Kieran didn't react. Amy kept logging in information. Finally, Kieran said, "I know a lot about computers. Probably more than anyone in town."

"No kidding? That's cool."

Another long silence, during which Kieran tried on a purple wool beret. The color looked terrific with the teen's dark coloring and Amy was considering telling her so when Kieran said, without looking away from her image in the mirror, "I saw your sign in the window. That you need part-time help."

"Yeah." She tried not to sound as pleased as she suddenly felt. "The only problem is, we're going to need somebody who isn't afraid of computers. Say, you wouldn't be interested in working some after school, would you?"

Kieran was now wrapping a serape around her shoulders and studying the effect. "Gee, I don't know."

"Of course, we'd want you to wear some of the clothes from the shop," Amy said. "You know, strictly to advertise. You could pick out what you like yourself."

Kieran touched a patchwork skirt draped dramatically across the corner of the mirror and said, "Yeah?"

Amy closed out her computer file and came around the counter. "Wow, you've got a terrific eye. I never noticed how well that skirt and that serape go together. Want to try it?"

SAM WAS SHARING his hammock with Amy that evening when they heard heavy footsteps coming up the deck of the cottage. The footsteps didn't sound like Grace's, so Amy turned her head to see who it was. Sam opened one eye and peered out, his tail beginning a tentative thump in anticipation of company.

Amy almost dumped the two of them on the deck when Jon's face appeared at the top of the steps.

She was sitting upright, waiting for the hammock to stop its erratic swaying, when she noticed the thunderous expression on his face.

"Cousin Jimmy said you were a meddler," he said. "He was right."

Amy felt a flash of irritation. She'd always thought Jimmy liked her, even if she hadn't been willing to go to bed with him during the six months they dated.

"Then he's a gossip," she snapped, swinging her

legs over the edge of the hammock and standing to confront him. "Meddling in what?"

"You had no right to hire my niece without my consent."

"Oh." She liked him angry, she decided. The fire in his eyes and the tough set of his mouth were as appealing as the unflappable cool he exuded most of the time. "I didn't?"

"No, you damn well didn't."

"Well, then, I apologize. I want to hire your niece. Okay?"

Her serenity had no effect on his irascibility. When he spoke, he was still growling. "No, it's not okay. I had plans of my own."

She waited. There had never been much arguing in her family and she discovered she liked the feel of this. The way adrenaline cranked up the body's responses a notch, the notion that people were saying what they thought, consequences be damned. She found that far less scary than the way her own family covered up whatever emotions raged beneath the surface. She realized she was smiling.

Jon wasn't. "She's going to work at the bakery. The way Costas kids have always done."

"I see. What if she would prefer to work for me?"

"She's a kid. She damn well doesn't always get what she wants."

She put her hands on his shoulders and backed him into one of the deck chairs.

"What the—"

"Give me a minute here," she said. Then she snapped her fingers, a command Sam responded to, if reluctantly. "Sam, keep an eye on him till I get back. Don't let him move."

Sam yawned and stationed himself in front of Jon, barely a hand's breadth from his knees.

"Is this dog going to bite me?" he called after her as she went into her cottage.

"Sam, use force only if necessary."

She wasn't sure if Jon was a beer man or a wine man, but she decided most men in a temper weren't in the mood to hold the stem of a wineglass between their fingers. So she popped the top on a couple of beers and took them out to the deck. She put one in Jon's hand, sat opposite him in the matching deck chair and said, "At ease, Sam."

Sam whined appreciatively and slithered into a puddle of sandy fur, covering the tips of Jon's feet with his head and the tips of Amy's feet with his backside.

"Now, you want to tell me why this is really bugging you?" she asked.

He slugged back about a quarter of the beer, gave the can a sour look and said, "I hate beer."

"If you're looking for another apology..." She shook her head.

His frown deepened. "Your watchdog is lying on my feet."

"Sam has extremely discriminating taste. He doesn't lie on just anyone's feet."

"Fine. I'm honored."

He sounded irritated, but Amy suspected he was having a hard time holding on to the anger that had brought him here. She took a lazy swallow of her beer and decided to wait for him to answer her question. He steamed for a bit first.

"She was supposed to start at the bakery on Monday. I told her that earlier this week."

"Ah. So she's going behind your back."

"Trying to. She'll find out it doesn't work."

"She's too old for you to control, Jon."

"The hell she is! I'm her uncle and if I don't do it, it's damn certain nobody else is going to." He downed more beer, then grimaced. "This stuff tastes like day-old dishwater."

"Remember being fifteen, Jon?"

She saw from the flash of guilt on his face that he knew exactly what she meant.

"Now, don't start that."

"Do you? I'm not sure I did, until Kieran walked into my shop today. But I watched her, the way she walked around the perimeter of the store. And I remembered how fragile everything felt when I was that age—knowing, somehow, that I could louse everything up if I took the wrong step, but never quite sure which step was the right one." She eased one bare foot out from under Sam's rump and used it to rub the dog's back. "God, that was a lousy time for me."

"I know," Jon said, some of the bite gone out of his voice. "But she's spinning out of control, and I care too much to let her ruin her life. She doesn't do a damn thing she's supposed to. And I've only got a few months. If she's at the bakery, where I can keep an eye on her..." He raised one hand in a gesture of futility.

"She certainly strikes me as the type who'll respond well to the crackdown of authority," Amy said and saw from the expression on his face that Jon knew what she meant. "She probably already resents you. Why not go ahead and really give her a reason to despise you?"

"Okay, Dr. Spock, what's your recommendation?"

"She might be better off in a place where she feels free to...blossom in her own way," Amy said. "If she's under your thumb every day, she's only going to make it her business to challenge you."

Jon drained the last of his beer and smashed the can in his fist. "In other words, I'm such an ogre that she's going to fight me all the way."

She smiled at him. "In other words, I think you're all she has of a parent right now."

"I'm not her parent. I didn't ask for this, you know."

"Nevertheless, you're stuck with it. And I doubt if she trusts parents very much."

"Yeah. Thank you very much, Nick."

"But Grace and I could be her friends."

"You think? You think anybody could be friends with a kid who doesn't wash her hair and wears a ring in her nose?"

Amy smiled. "I gave her some different clothes to wear to work. Stuff from the shop. I think she got into it."

"Stuff without holes in it?"

"I told her she'd have to wash her hair, too."

Jon's eyes grew wide. "And she took the job anyway?"

"Well, we do have a computer."

"Ah. Well, no wonder the bakery came in a distant second."

"Give us a chance, Jon."

"So Jimmy was right. You *are* meddling."

She grinned at the hint of humor in his voice. "It's my nature."

"I'll consider myself warned."

They sat in silence for a few moments, then Jon slid his feet out from under Sam's muzzle and stood. He walked to the edge of the deck and leaned his elbows on the railing. "If I lived right here on the water, I might never go inside."

She joined him, pausing a moment to absorb the soothing rhythm of the surf. Whitecaps glowed in the moonlight. "I know. When I went away to college, I thought I was going to go crazy."

"Maybe that's why I had to get out of New York."

"But you said you're going back."

"Maybe. Or maybe not."

"You're thinking of staying, after all?"

"No. Just looking at other options. Maybe a place in the Keys. Some fishing. Some financial consulting."

"You could do that here. I'll bet Dad would help you get started." She took in the way the moonlight accented his strong features. "This feeds me, too. The ceaselessness of it. It reminds me that there's some kind of rhythm to it all."

"You believe that?"

"Yeah. I do." She grinned. "Even though I sometimes want to get in there and adjust the beat."

"Would you change the rhythm right now?"

She thought of a needy teenager and an equally needy man, using up his life buried in a city where money was seen as the ultimate reward. She smiled. "No. Right now, you're probably exactly where you're supposed to be."

He turned toward her, bringing his arm in touch with hers. "Right here, on this deck, in this moonlight, with this woman?"

Her mouth went dry and the beat of her heart accelerated to warp speed. That wasn't what she'd been thinking at all. And now Jon was smiling faintly, and she felt suddenly helpless against all the old feelings his presence had resurrected.

"Oh. That. Well…"

"Is there a rhythm to this, Amy?" The tips of his fingers brushed her elbow; sensations swept her up like the crash of a wave in the rough sea. Exhilarated and fearful at once, she tried to move away from his touch. But the brush of his fingertips had captured her in their tender rhythm.

"Jon, I…"

He raised his fingers, drew them to her face, traced the deep hollow below her cheekbone. Amy closed her eyes, wondering if he was right. Life's sure and steady advance had brought them here, so who was she to say it was wrong?

He whispered her name.

She leaned into him, felt the heat from his chest, the puffs of warm breath as his face grew closer, came lower. The way she had dreamed of it so many times, so many times when she'd believed it would never happen, *should* never happen. And all because of…

Lisa.

Swallowing hard, she pulled herself back to harsh reality. She saw—for an instant before he sensed her change in mood—the dreamy lethargy on his face, saw the way his lips readied themselves for hers.

Good Lord, what was she doing?

If there really was rhyme and reason to life, she had to remember that Jon's destiny wasn't with her, but with her sister. Lisa needed Jon as much as he needed her. For heaven's sake, Lisa even had the experience to help him deal with a troubled girl like Kieran.

She backed away, trembling.

Jon was frowning again. "Guess I'd better go."

She nodded. "I'm, uh, glad you came by. Glad we're in agreement about Kieran."

For a moment, he looked inclined to disagree once again. Then he simply nodded and turned away. When he reached the bottom of the steps, he looked up. The ache in Amy was familiar and she told herself it would go away.

"So, I'll see you around?" he said. "Tomorrow, maybe? For our jog?"

"Well, maybe not. My leg, you know. I overdid it."

He nodded. "Sure. Well, in the morning, at least."

She nodded, too, wondering if she could somehow convince Grace to go for their breakfast rolls. Given the history there, she doubted it.

She watched him walk down the beach in the direction of town and cursed her weakness. She'd let all those foolish old longings get in the way of good sense. In the way of doing what she knew was right.

Lisa popped into her mind again. Not today's Lisa, the self-assured woman with the suffer-no-fools voice on the answering machine. But the exuberant Lisa from twenty years ago, the one who giggled on command and collected bad jokes and sand dollars. The Lisa who had been one of her two best friends.

Amy watched as Jon disappeared down the beach. Her face still tingled with the memory of his touch and she allowed herself to imagine what it would have been like if his lips had touched hers. The ringing of the telephone saved her from that journey, and she ran inside, grabbing the receiver like a lifeline.

"Amy?" She recognized the voice instantly. "It's Lisa."

## CHAPTER SEVEN

JON WALKED the long way home, straight down the beach until he hit the broad sidewalk separating the businesses along Gulfview from the beach. Then, instead of turning toward town, he kept walking, stepped off the sidewalk when it ended and found the path through the beginnings of the salt marsh.

He needed time to analyze what was going on with Amy.

His career in the stock market had taught him that he could analyze anything and, thereby, come to control it.

His analysis wasn't getting very far. The facts seemed simple enough. She was an attractive woman to whom he'd felt drawn for as long as he could remember. She was available and so was he. As relationships go, it all sounded pretty straight-forward up to that point.

But the other facts—the ones he told himself shouldn't be relevant—that kept tripping him up. The fact that she was the sister of his ex-wife. The fact his parents hadn't liked him marrying outside the Greek community the first time. Finally, there was the fact he had more on his plate right now than he could handle, without messing up his head with a woman like Amy Hardaway. A woman who wouldn't let him keep a comfortable emotional distance.

And therein lay the biggest dragon under the bed. He'd loused up too many times because he was neurotic about letting anyone get too close. He couldn't commit because he still wanted what he'd wanted as a kid—all the freedom and none of the ties.

Was he really willing to add the spirited and guileless Amy to the list of people he'd drawn close only to push away at a critical moment?

Apparently.

Thank heaven she had better sense than he had, or he would probably be out there kissing her right now.

He wished he was.

He wished he was holding her lithe body close to his, touching that lush, silky hair, feeling those full lips.

By the time he reached the docks at the mouth of Alligator Creek, he was no closer to making sense of the way Amy appealed to him than he'd been in that moment when kissing her had seemed more important than drawing his next breath.

The docks were well lit, especially around Jimmy's boats, and he heard the boisterous voices of his cousins. Grateful for a distraction—and for an excuse not to go home—Jon walked over to see what was going on. Jimmy, George and Gus were hanging over the engine of one of the old tubs, arguing about the propeller shaft. They smelled of grease and beer. His *theo* Nikos sat in a deck chair on the dock, feet on one of the damp, barnacled pilings.

"Are they in any condition to be working on an engine?" Jon asked his uncle.

Nikos waved a hand at his three sons. "Ah, they play. Boys must play."

Jimmy stuck his head out of the engine area belowdecks. His face was streaked with grease and his grin was wide. "Jon, we need your help. Come. Four heads are better than one."

Jon held up his hands under the glare of one of the overhead lights. "See these hands? Aunt Aurelia will have all four of our heads if I get grease on them. I have dough to knead, you philistines."

His cousins laughed and ribbed him about women's work. Jon enjoyed the warm feeling that came over him. Nothing like the thin camaraderie he'd sometimes felt when he went out with people after work in New York. He realized he hadn't thought of Bailey Bookman in weeks, and he'd always thought of Book as a real friend, someone with whom he shared a bond.

Thinking about it now, Jon realized he'd always felt—beneath the friendship—the threat of competition, the possibility that some of his colleagues—maybe even Book—might be willing to stab him in the back if it furthered their careers.

Looking back, he remembered walking around New York feeling that something was missing in his life. Now, standing here on the dock beneath a starry sky, with the pungent scent of the sea hanging heavy in the air, laughing with his cousins, he wondered if that something had been home and family.

He almost laughed out loud. His encounter with Amy was making him romanticize this moment.

He knew this feeling would pass in the face of reality—Kieran and the bakery and his interfering parents. The way his feelings for Amy would pass, too.

He leaned against a piling near Nikos and tossed insults back and forth with his cousins for another hour, until everyone good-naturedly agreed that the boat would either run better than ever the next morning, or sink before it reached deep water. Then the five of them walked home through the quiet streets. Jimmy and George dropped off first, then Gus two blocks later. For the final block, it was only Jon and his uncle Nikos. People called out from their porches, greeting Nikos, asking if the boys had got the boat up and running. The interruptions irritated Jon, but he noted that Nikos seemed to take pleasure in the concern of his friends and neighbors.

As they ambled down a quiet street where everyone had apparently turned in for the night, Nikos faced Jon and said, "So, you wonder sometimes if you will ever be one of us again. Or if you even want to."

Surprised at the observation, Jon looked at his uncle and wondered how he knew.

Nikos smiled. "I know. Aurelia and Leda, they are not the only ones who know things without being told. And I know, the day comes when you are glad to be home."

"Am I home? Really?"

"You had dreams of more."

"Don't we all?" Then Jon felt guilty, knowing his comment belittled the life Nikos had chosen— or settled for. All his life, Jon had assumed his father and uncle had settled. Coming to the United States as children with their immigrant parents, they had done the best they could. But they'd never gotten rich, and Jon had always interpreted that as meaning the American Dream had passed them by. Here they were, past retirement age, and still working long hours. What kind of dreams had they laid to rest over the years?

"Ah, my boy," Nikos said with a gentle sigh, "I have more than I ever dreamed."

They paused in front of Jon's parents' house. The low light from the wrought-iron pole in the yard softened the signs of age and hard work in Uncle Nikos's face, and Jon saw something he hadn't stopped to notice before. Contentment.

"I have fine boys, many fine grandchildren," Nikos said. "I have a wife who still puts up with me, and a soft bed waiting. I have friends, many friends who would come for me if I call. I have workdays full of laughter, and satisfaction from knowing my labor feeds people."

Nikos clapped him on the shoulder in the way men sometimes did when they felt moved to embrace one another. "More than I ever dreamed."

With a wave, Nikos continued toward the soft bed and the wife who still put up with him. Jon watched him, wondering how his own ledger of assets would stack up against his uncle's ledger of loyal friends, loving family and pleasure in day-to-day existence.

Hurricane Beach, he realized, was full of people who were successful by his uncle's standards.

Amy Hardaway came to mind, lying in her hammock with her dog Sam and the moonlit beach for her entertainment. He turned and went into the house. Where did Amy fit in his struggle to find his own contentment? he wondered. And should he even be trying to figure that out?

AMY'S HEART had been pounding hard before she even heard Lisa's voice. What, exactly, had been going on out there with Jon Costas?

But when she realized Lisa was on the phone, guilt cut through her.

What on earth had she been thinking, standing there in the dark with her ex-brother-in-law, shivering at the touch of his fingers? The shivers skittered through her again, just thinking about his fingertips grazing her cheek.

"Lisa! Oh! Goodness! You called." *And you're*

*dithering. Lisa didn't call to hear you dither. She probably hates that about you.* She forced herself to calm down. At least outwardly. "How are you?"

"I'm fine, Amy. Is anything wrong there?"

Drawing a deep breath, she told Lisa about the anniversary celebration and asked her to come home during Spring Break to discuss it. "Megan will be here, too, and we just thought it would be...nice."

She had to fight to keep from saying "like old times." Somehow, she knew that would put her sister off.

"You don't really need me there," Lisa said. "Not just to plan a party. You and Megan can call me when she's there. We could talk then."

"But it would be so much easier if we were all together," Amy said, feeling an increased urgency to get her sister down here. If Lisa saw Jon, if Jon saw Lisa, surely there would be no more danger of caresses in the moonlight. Amy would be forced to put all those adolescent cravings back in a tightly lidded box. "We want to make sure you're happy with the plans, too. So—"

"Whatever the two of you decide will be fine," Lisa said, crisp and businesslike. "Besides, if I'm coming down later this year, how much sense does it make for me to come now, too?"

Feeling guilty, grasping at the only ammunition she had, Amy said, "I didn't want to tell you this, but I think Mom and Dad are having problems."

"What do you mean?"

"Problems." The words stuck in her throat. "They're talking about divorce."

"What?"

"I heard them. They've been arguing. You should hear them."

"Amy, are you sure you haven't…let this thing get a little bigger in your mind than it actually is?"

"Ask Megan, if you don't believe me," Amy replied. "She said Mom was crying the last time she called. And Mom and Dad were at the bank, looking through their safe-deposit box and talking about how to divide their property."

"Tell me this, then," Lisa said. "If they're thinking about divorce, what in heaven's name are we doing planning a fiftieth anniversary celebration?"

It was the same question Megan had asked, and it deserved a reasonable answer. Amy did her best. "Because we need to do something to make them come to their senses. We can't just sit back and let them…let them…divorce!"

"Amy, it's none of our business."

"You think I'm meddling." Amy tried not to let her irritation show. She was growing tired of hearing this from everyone.

"That's your word, not mine," Lisa said. "But I do think our parents have the right to work out their problems however they see fit."

With a tightening in her throat, Amy knew nothing she could say would help her sister understand that family helped family. Lisa had obviously lost all sense of family. She didn't seem to care one whit that their parents might be on the verge of separation and heartbreak. It was as if Lisa had been alone, unconnected, for so long that she could no longer feel the pain. Amy felt the sting of tears in her eyes.

Despairing of finding a way to bridge the gap between herself and her sister, Amy asked, "Don't you care?"

She heard the impatience when Lisa said, "Of course I care. But it isn't my job to fix the world."

Stung by the sharpness in her sister's tone, Amy swallowed her tears and floundered for a reply. Something to recapture Lisa's heart, or at least to keep her on the phone a little longer. She could think of only one thing, and right now the topic of Jon Costas gave her twinges of guilt.

"Why don't you call me back when Megan's there and we'll—"

Panic. The conversation was ending, and God knows if she would get a second chance. *Do something. Quick!* "Did you hear Jon Costas is back?"

There. Nothing to feel guilty about. Although the long silence on the other end of the line gave her a few more moments to experience the unwelcome memory of Jon's nearness and warmth.

"Really? Back for good?"

Aha! That was real interest, wasn't it? More interest than she'd shown for their parents' problems.

"Actually, I'm not sure. But he's helping his

folks get the bakery on firm footing again. And helping raise Nick's daughter."

"*Jon* is?"

Amy smiled, pleased with herself for capturing Lisa's attention. She filled her sister in on the details of Nick's relapse and Jon's return, noting smugly that Lisa didn't bother to point out that news of her ex-husband was none of Amy's business.

"If you came at Spring Break, you'd get a chance to see Jon again. Catch up. I know he'd enjoy it."

"You have my permission to fill him in for me, Amy. I don't think I need to come back to Hurricane Beach, not to straighten out Mom and Dad and certainly not for a bit of auld lang syne with my ex-husband."

But when Amy hung up a few minutes later, she smiled at Sam. "I was right. Lisa is interested. A reconciliation with her ex-husband is exactly what she needs."

The idea definitely made Amy miserable.

KIERAN'S FIRST WEEK on the job provided exactly the distraction Amy needed.

Instead of thinking about how much she missed her afternoon runs on the beach with Jon Costas, Amy flitted about making sure Kieran felt comfortable and learned the ropes at Rêve Rags. She showed her how to log in clothing brought in by consigners, and how to stock new items. She showed her how to encourage shoppers and how to ring up purchases. She introduced her to the computer system and listened while the teenager explained easier ways to keep track of sales and payouts.

And for minutes at a time, Amy didn't think about Jon. She forgot about the way she felt when Jon was around—the racing heart, the rush of heat through her body, the skin that suddenly seemed to have a million and one nerve endings. And she certainly didn't allow herself to worry about the fireworks that were certain to erupt if Lisa found out about those feelings.

For minutes at a time, those things didn't occupy her mind. And for that she was grateful.

Because at the end of the day, when Rêve Rags closed and the spring evenings grew longer, Amy thought of nothing else. Even the problems of Helene and Merrick faded in the face of this obsession for a man she couldn't have.

Amy had painted herself into a corner, with no way out.

Grace knew it, too. Her partner gave her that sly, told-you-so look at every opportunity. That was another reason Amy was grateful for Kieran's presence. At least for those few hours after school, Grace had to put a lid on the looks and pointed remarks.

"You are remarkably quiet for someone who has so many schemes going," Grace said one afternoon. "What gives?"

"I'm a contemplative person," Amy said, looking

out the window, hoping to see Kieran coming down the sidewalk.

Grace grunted as she draped a triple strand of ceramic beads around the neck of a cotton sweater and stood back to judge the effect. "Good afternoon for a run."

Amy didn't reply. She hadn't run all week. And no matter how many times she had explained about pulling her calf muscle the week before, Grace continued to imply it had something to do with not wanting to see Jon Costas.

"When are you going to admit it, girl? You stirred up more than you could handle with that ex-brother-in-law of yours, didn't you?"

"I don't know what you're talking about."

"Uh-huh. That lie rolled off your tongue like you do it every day of your life." Grace tried on one of the hats that had come in the day before, a big, floppy-brimmed number with a madras band. "Those Costas men can hook you in. I know what I'm talking about. And I know the signs when I see them."

"Drop it, Grace. Here comes Kieran."

Grace peered out the window. "I must admit, you're working miracles with her."

Kieran seemed to drag the sunshine into the shop with her. She smiled as she greeted Grace and Amy and breezed through to the back of the shop to get rid of her book bag. She wore a flippy little skirt Amy had set aside for her. And the afternoon before, she'd taken her tangle of hair to the shop down the street. Her dark, straight hair was now cropped neat and close to her head, a shining cap that set off her dark-lashed eyes and flawless olive complexion.

"What do you think?" Kieran asked, anticipation making it hard for her to stand still.

"You're a new woman," Amy said.

Grace smiled at the girl and pretended to study her critically. "I think *Seventeen* magazine is looking for its next cover girl."

Kieran laughed, her cheeks growing rosy with the compliments. "Thanks, guys. So, did you save all the sales for me to key in?"

Amy pointed to the stack of receipts. "Your mop and broom, Cinderella."

Kieran's eyes lit up as she swung onto the stool behind the counter. "Cool."

Amy smiled, watching their new part-timer. In just a few days, she was shaping up as a near-perfect employee. She listened carefully, almost eagerly, to everything Amy and Grace told her. She was quiet and attentive when customers came in. An urge came over Amy, the urge to tell Jon about the difference in his niece, to ask if things were changing at home, too.

A flurry of customers kept them all hopping for the next half hour. And just when things were quieting down again, a tall, distinguished-looking man in a suit walked in and looked around.

"Welcome to Rêve Rags," Amy said with a

bright smile. "I'm Amy. Can I help you find something?"

"Ah, Miss Hardaway. My name is Palmer Boyce."

He extended his hand and she shook it. A salesman, she supposed, although he was awfully expensively dressed for most of the men who came in trying to sell office supplies or new software or advertising on their radio stations. Better dressed and more mature, too. Palmer Boyce looked to be in his mid-fifties, although certainly attractive with his tall, lean build and well-tended tan.

"I wondered, Miss Hardaway, if I might have a few minutes of your time. I have some information I believe will interest you. Information about your parents' financial security. Their future together."

An attorney. Amy's heart did a flip-flop. Of course. She didn't want to hear this. She wanted to send him packing, as if that would make everything better. See what happened when she let things slide, didn't take things into her own hands right away? An attorney. Probably here to ask her to testify— against her own father, for heaven's sake!—as to Merrick's drinking. Why, this smooth-talking, good-looking scoundrel had probably put the entire idea of divorce into Helene's mind in the first place.

Amy's eyes narrowed. Well, she could certainly set Palmer Boyce straight. In a heartbeat.

"Fine," she said, the single clipped word expressing all her contempt.

He looked over her shoulder. "Perhaps a little more privacy would be in order. I'd gladly buy you a cup of tea or coffee."

He gestured down the street, in the direction of Java Joe's. She nodded. He smiled. A very sincere smile. Amy hated him already.

"You won't be sorry."

*No,* she thought, itching to take advantage of this opportunity to set things right for her parents. *But you might be.*

# CHAPTER EIGHT

ANOTHER SOLITARY JOG. Jon grumbled to himself as he finished an hour running against a stiff ocean wind, with his legs painfully tight and his mood worse than it had been all week.

And that was saying something.

Every day, he kept expecting Amy to show up for what he had come to think of as "their" run. And every day, she disappointed him.

Amy. How was he supposed to get her out of his system if she made such a point of avoiding him? Whoever came up with that old out-of-sight, out-of-mind business had obviously never encountered Amy Hardaway. He hadn't seen her in days except for the moments it took her each morning to dash in and out of the bakery. And with each hour that passed, his memories of her grew more vivid. More distracting.

Her hair, the way it drifted down her back like a blush-and-amber waterfall—unless she had it tied up for their run, when it clung to her cheeks and her neck and her forehead, caught by her perspiration. Her skin, as pale and translucent in the moonlight as fine china, flushed like a ripe peach after an hour of exertion in the sun. Her legs, her endless legs, the knees lightly dusted with freckles.

"Dammit!" He kicked viciously at a length of seaweed-covered driftwood.

If the way she looked had been the only thing troubling him, he could get over it. There were plenty of good-looking women, even in Hurricane Beach. But what really kept coming back to haunt him were the things she'd talked about when they'd been together. Her enthusiasm for her shop, her loyalty to Grace, her almost childlike enjoyment of the afternoons they spent plodding up and down the coast. The way she stopped to wrinkle up her face over a jellyfish washed up on the shore, or to turn her face up in delight when a flock of sea gulls screeched at them from overhead.

Just watching her at times like those gave him a rush. He wondered how different things might be now if it had been Amy, all those years ago. He cursed softly. Probably the outcome would have been no better, because few people could be more different than Amy and he. Her innocent joy in life, her enthusiasm for everything around her, even the easygoing way she tolerated his family were all things he admired in her, but certainly weren't traits he shared.

Then there were the things she'd said the night he'd gone over to blast her for hiring Kieran. Amy had made him look at things differently. He'd begun to realize that he didn't have to save his niece single-handedly, and that the biggest gift he might be able to give the girl was simply to let her know he was there for her.

But to do that, he would have to actually be *here* for her. He would have to stay in Hurricane Beach.

Maybe, as Amy had said that last night they spoke, he was right where he was supposed to be. Here in Hurricane Beach, learning to slow down, trying to find some of the things that had made his pop and Nikos so successful. He wanted to talk more about those things. With Amy.

And, dammit, she didn't have the common courtesy to even show up. As if she'd read his mind and knew as well as he that he could only complicate her life. Knowing that had obviously given her the strength to stay away. Too bad it hadn't done the same for Jon.

Enough of this. He would find her.

He went to her shop, recognizing even in his haste the way the display window at Rêve Rags reflected Amy's personality. It was filled with brightly colored clothing, all of it soft and very trendy. Beach toys—plastic buckets and shovels and old-fashioned striped beach balls—completed the display. Bright and fun, just like Amy.

Jon stormed through the open front door as his niece was helping Grace Kingsolver move a rack of shorts across the store. He froze, amazed at how Kieran looked. When had this happened? he wondered, taking in the sleek haircut and the cute little skirt that had replaced her ragged jeans. Goodbye matted, unwashed hair. Goodbye nose ring.

*Thank you, Amy, for meddling.*

When Kieran spotted him, however, her smile dissolved. Her sulky frown reappeared. "What are you doing here?"

"Looking for Amy."

Grace and Kieran exchanged a look, one of those inner-circle looks that women shared when they had no intention of telling a man what he had a perfect right to know. Jon's irritation grew.

"She went out," Grace said.

"Where?"

"I'm not sure."

"For how long?"

Grace's smile was sweet but secretive. "I really don't know. You're welcome to wait."

*Wait, hell.* He thanked them and left then stalked down the street, stopping in at the Green Market and the bank, even the seafood market. How far could she have gone in the middle of a workday?

Of course, she was accustomed to taking an hour off in the afternoon to jog with him. Since she was no longer jogging, what was she doing with that time?

Telling himself that it was none of his damn business, that there was no reason to get himself so worked up, Jon continued his determined hunt along Gulfview, peering into every shop.

Finally, there she was, sitting in the window of

Java Joe's, sipping something dark and creamy. Wearing something gauzy, the color of the first leaves of spring, wide at the neck so her delicate collarbone showed. Wide at the neck so it threatened to slip off one shoulder. She was listening intently to whatever was being said by a dapper-looking gentleman across the table from her. A stranger in a thousand-dollar suit, his graying temples razor cut by someone who charged fifty dollars for the ten-minute job, if Jon knew the signs of money. And he did.

For an instant, Jon almost acted on the urge to storm into Java Joe's and demand to know what she was doing in a cozy little tête-à-tête with this smoothie who was old enough to be her father. Is this where she'd been all week, when he'd been out there sweating by himself, plaguing himself with thoughts of her?

Then he saw her eyes, staring straight at him. He'd been caught. Caught gaping at her like some damn fool kid with a crush.

He whirled and stomped off, reminding himself he had no business concerning himself with the comings and goings of his ex-sister-in-law. He'd already fallen in love with his quota of Hardaway sisters. And if he'd loused it up, that was his tough luck.

Love offered no second chances when it came to picking the right sister.

AMY LOOKED UP from her cup of coffee, intending to study the face of this man who claimed so convincingly to have her parents' best interests at heart. But what she saw, over his shoulder, was the frowning face of Jon Costas.

Amy choked on her caffe latte.

It was the expression on Jon's face that closed her throat and made her breath catch in the split second before he wheeled and disappeared, his brooding eyes filled with a look that was almost...possessive.

Equally captivating were his damp hair, his sweat-streaked tank shirt, his sun-bronzed shoulders.

"Are you all right?" Palmer Boyce, representative of the Silver Sands Development Company, reached across the tiny round table and lightly placed a hand on her wrist.

His touch felt a little bit clammy. Amy reluctantly dragged her thoughts away from Jon and back to the unwelcome news Palmer Boyce had brought.

"Yes," she said, picking up a napkin and blotting her lips as an excuse for pulling away from his touch. "Fine. Now, what you're telling me is that Silver Sands has already made an offer to my parents."

"That's correct," Palmer said, managing to sound both friendly and official at the same time. "Quite a substantial offer."

Palmer pulled a gold Cross pen from his inside breast pocket and wrote a figure on his napkin.

Not *a* figure, actually. Eight of them.

Amy almost knocked over her coffee reaching for the napkin. She crumpled it and shoved it into the roomy pocket of her dress. "You're not serious."

Palmer smiled and nodded. "Very serious. And I feel I can tell you this in good faith, Miss Hardaway—may I call you Amy?"

With visions of dollar signs dancing in her head, Amy nodded without thinking. Her parents were well off, but this...

"I want you to know that Silver Sands is prepared to go higher, if necessary."

"Higher?"

He nodded. Amy's heart was pounding.

"But why?"

"Surely you must know, Miss—Amy—that Hurricane Beach is the only substantial stretch of undeveloped land along the entire Gulf Coast." He leaned forward, his intensity generating sparks in the air. "We believe Hurricane Beach, with its reputation for affluent visitors and low-key attractions, can be the cornerstone for tourism in the Panhandle in the next century."

Although she knew precisely how carefully scripted Palmer Boyce's pitch must be, Amy found herself reacting just as he no doubt hoped she would. As a businessperson.

She could envision the bustling but restrained resort Hurricane Beach could become with the changes Palmer Boyce had outlined. A few tastefully elegant high-rise hotels. Condominiums tucked discreetly among the dunes. A lush, well-manicured golf course. Riding trails.

And, of course, visitors. Visitors with lots of money to spend in the little shops along Gulfview.

Shops like Rêve Rags.

The businessperson in Amy got excited over the picture growing in her head. But the lifelong resident in her began to rebel at the idea of hordes of tourists trampling the dunes and littering the powdery sand and polluting their private little stretch of turquoise gulf.

"I know this is a lot to digest," Palmer said, his voice intimately soothing. "And I know, of course, that you're a smart enough entrepreneur to want to think it over from every angle before you decide."

"Decide? What do I have to decide?" she asked. "It's not my property."

"For the sake of your parents, Amy, I'm afraid the decision *may* rest with you."

"What are you talking about?"

Palmer shook his head and stared pensively into his empty coffee mug. "Your parents don't seem to agree on the issue of selling."

Amy's heart plummeted. Of course. She should have seen it. Palmer Boyce had stirred up all this turmoil with his offer. She wanted to sling the remains of her coffee all over his red-and-cream silk tie.

"I'm afraid the strain of this disagreement is too

much for Helene and Merrick," he said. "They need guidance."

"Maybe they need you to go away and leave them alone," Amy said between clenched teeth.

"I wish that were possible, Amy. But I can tell you in all confidence that, if I do that, someone else will come along." Palmer smiled gently. "I know how this will sound, but I must say it anyway. Because I like Helene and Merrick. But I would rather be the one to guide them through this than leave it to...some of the other kinds of people they might encounter if they don't do business with Silver Sands."

Amy wanted to tell him that Merrick Hardaway had played hardball with the best in the business, before he retired. She wanted to tell him to take his eight-figure offer and shove it in his Italian-leather briefcase.

Then he said, "Your parents deserve this kind of financial security. But more than that, they need help if they are to get through this with their relationship intact."

The weight of his words began to bear down on Amy's shoulders. He was right, of course. They were fighting. Talking divorce. And now that she knew why, Amy owed it to them—to the whole family, really—to help.

And apparently, even a stranger could see that Amy was the perfect daughter for the job.

Naturally.

PALMER BOYCE WATCHED her walk back to her shop, her step considerably slower than it had been a half hour earlier, and felt confident she would do exactly what he wanted.

He'd seen both the light in those pale green eyes when he'd talked about growth potential for local businesses and the crushing concern when he'd dumped the guilt in her lap for her parents' discord. Yes, Amy Hardway was precisely who he needed to help him get the job done.

And get the job done he must. He'd heard from the people upstairs just yesterday and the pressure was on to close the deal for the Hardaway property. But no matter how much pressure Palmer applied, the couple couldn't seem to agree. It had occurred to Palmer that a daughter who owned a business in Hurricane Beach might be convinced of the wisdom of accepting Silver Sands's offer.

Failing that, he had one more trump card to play. Helene Hardaway.

He knew she was the holdout. He also knew things were tense between her and Merrick. And she was just enough older than Palmer to be flattered if his professional attention should turn a little more personal.

Yes, his next tactic would be charming the lovely Helene Hardaway. So subtly, of course, that Merrick Hardaway would never find out what was going on.

Palmer thought he might just go ahead and lay the groundwork for that next item in his bag of tricks.

THE SURF WAS CALM and the sky the palest blue, but the acrylic scene Amy created on her canvas wasn't.

In the scene coming from her brush strokes, the water roiled and broke, crashing violently on the sand. Murky grays and dangerous violets had robbed her painted sky of most of its blue. The scene looked the way she felt—disturbed, fearful, unsettled in the extreme.

The gazebo where she sat and painted was her favorite place along the beach. Halfway between her cottage and Sea Haven, the gingerbread-trimmed gazebo belonged with a beach house that hadn't yet sold since its owner passed away six months earlier. This far out of town, the beach was typically deserted.

She painted furiously until dusk robbed her of light. Then she set her canvas aside, wiped her fingers on the smock she wore and sat back, eyes closed, hoping to discover that her turmoil had diminished.

She heard nothing but gulls and surf until a voice came to her through the softness of twilight. "I'd heard this was the prettiest part of the beach. I see why now."

Jon's voice, surprisingly, calmed her. She didn't open her eyes, but she felt herself smiling. Strange that he should affect her this way, when he was a major part of her distress. "I'd heard you were a smooth talker. I see why now."

She sensed him step into the gazebo, pick up her canvas and sit beside her on the bench. Although his physical presence suddenly filled her, overpowered her, it didn't diminish the peacefulness his arrival had brought.

"Hmm. I take it you're upset."

She opened her eyes and looked at the painting he held. At this moment, she couldn't even remember feeling all the emotions that had surfaced in her work. "So it appears."

He leaned the painting against the wall of the gazebo and angled to face her. He was close. Close enough to touch. Close enough to spark many unsisterly feelings.

"Why have you been avoiding me?" he said, his voice soft but demanding.

Both the soft and the demanding sparked a response in Amy, sent sensations prickling along the surface of her flesh.

"I don't know what you're talking about," she said as firmly as she could, given that her lungs refused to fill with air and her heart was thumping too hard to be contained by the walls of her chest.

"That's a crock," he said, inching closer.

She could smell him now, that beguiling scent of spices and yeast and salt air and man that was distinctly Jon Costas.

*Your brother-in-law,* she reminded herself.

*Ex,* came the rejoinder. *Not anymore. Not for years.*

*Tell that to Lisa.*

"You've quit coming out to run," Jon said. "You dash into and out of the bakery before I can blink. For two weeks, you were underfoot every time I turned around, and suddenly you've vanished. I want to know why."

Some of her earlier agitation began to return. She knew why she'd been avoiding him, of course. But she could hardly tell him. She tried sounding firm and confident as she said, "Jon, you're out of line. You—"

"I know what I'm talking about. And I want you to answer me."

"I... Well... This is..."

"Okay," he said. "I'll tell you why."

He drew close enough now to put his hands on her shoulders. His hands were just strong enough, just gentle enough. Amy felt herself go weak—her knees, her breathing, even her heartbeat seemed to falter. Her brain sent out an alarm, but her body couldn't respond.

"This is what you're afraid of," he said.

As he lowered his lips to hers, and Amy felt herself willingly, eagerly, spiraling down the tunnel with him, her last rational thought was: He was absolutely right.

## CHAPTER NINE

JON HELD HER lightly for a moment, touching his lips to hers tentatively, and waited for her response.

He felt the reaction flare through her, a power surge that seared them both. He sensed her tense, but the instant of resistance vanished as quickly as it had come.

She then melted into his embrace, softened into his kiss. A tiny triumph cheered him—drowning out the warning cries his mind sounded—as he drew her sleek, lithe body more tightly against his. He allowed himself to linger over her lips. Velvety, full, they played back at him, giving generously of her sweetness. Jon touched the seam of her lips with his tongue and felt fire in his loins.

He almost backed off, the call of his body was so sharp, so sudden. The intensity frightened him.

But her breasts were high and firm against his chest and her arms wound so beguilingly around his neck. She was warm, pliant, making little sighs in her throat. He couldn't back away. Couldn't let her go. Instead, he held her more tightly, fighting his misgivings. If he buried himself in the warm recesses of her mouth, he told himself, if he nuzzled himself close enough against the giving tenderness of her lean body, his qualms would surely be reduced to nothing.

He raked his fingers through her hair and found it silky and lush, the way he had always imagined it. He cupped her head in one hand, angling her for a deeper kiss. His other hand he trailed down her back, feeling the tease of her long, loose curls.

Her fingers clutched at his shoulders, drawing a shiver from him.

When his caress reached the swell of her hip, a tiny cry rose from her chest. Her sound nudged him further from control. He longed to press his erection against her belly, to taste the crest of one of her breasts. The part of his mind that still functioned told him this stretch of beach was isolated, that he could take her, now, before he had time to think.

Before the fear could creep back in and take hold.

Just thinking of the fear brought it to the surface, and it suddenly had a name.

Commitment.

He tried to hold the thought at bay with a kiss more desperate, less controlled.

As if sensing the change in him, Amy suddenly tensed again, placing her hands between them, on his chest. Jon forced himself to loosen his hold. To drag his lips away from hers. She stepped away, knocking a jar of water and brushes to the wooden platform, holding one trembling hand to her chest. The other she slipped through her hair, pulling the tousled red-gold strands away from her flushed cheeks. She looked shell-shocked; Jon felt the same.

He tried to think what to say. Tried to remember what he had said to her, right before he'd kissed her. But his mind was a blank. He was operating on sheer physical instinct right now. He had never lost control this way, had never given himself so completely to his emotions.

Or to another person, he thought. Yet he hadn't felt crowded, or smothered, or trapped. Still, he shuddered.

"I think you'd better go." Her voice was the faintest of whispers, breathless. Not the kind of sound to encourage him to leave, or leave her alone.

But Jon knew she was right. If he didn't go...

He remembered, when his feet hit the sand, what he'd said to her. Something about knowing what it was she was afraid of. He smiled at his arrogance. He hadn't known, just a few short minutes ago, that this was something worthy of both their fear.

He turned to the gazebo, still smiling, and said, "If it's any consolation, I'm afraid of it, too."

IT TOOK AN HOUR for Amy to compose herself enough to pack up her supplies and walk back to her cottage. It took longer than that for her body to stop responding to the memory of Jon's demanding kiss.

Amy ignored Sam when she reached her house, walking straight through the living room to stash her canvas bag in her studio, then into the bathroom, where she intended to splash her still-heated face with cool water.

The face in the mirror caught her. The look in her eyes haunted her.

What had happened? One minute, she'd been a sane, rational human being, concerned with the feelings of others and governed by a strong sense of right and wrong. And the next, she'd been driven by needs that threatened to devour her. She had craved Jon in a way that she'd never craved a man before. The feelings were so powerful they'd overwhelmed everything else.

She hadn't once thought of Lisa.

She could feel the hunger deep inside her, ready to take hold of her again at the slightest urging.

"Remember what's important," she whispered to the troubled image in the mirror. "Remember Lisa."

COAST CLEAR, Kieran thought, watching as both Amy and Grace walked down the street on separate errands for the shop, one to the bank, the other to the copy shop for more consignment-contract forms. Quickly, she stepped behind the counter and logged onto the computer, hoping no customers would come in for the next few minutes.

Hardball had given her some pointers on how to check out the other capabilities of the store's system. Heart pounding, one eye on the door, she began using the commands she had copied from Hardball's message the night before. And in moments, an exciting new world began to open up on the small, square screen.

Local library records, which didn't interest her much. But the school, even the bank, all of them laid out in front of her were more fun than the most expensive computer game her old man had ever given her. Fingers trembling, the open front door forgotten, Kieran followed Hardball's directions, made a few wrong turns, backtracked. Hacking, Hardball called it. An experienced hacker, he said, could even get into top-secret government files. Kieran persevered, wanting her new on-line friend to be proud of her when they talked tonight.

Then the door to Oz opened. The Emerald City was hers.

She had accessed her school records.

There it was, all her grades, all the teachers' snotty little comments, her days absent, everything. Mouth dry, heart racing, she dragged the mouse down to her English grade for the previous term. The D that had gotten everybody's underpants in a knot. Holding her breath, she typed a B over the offending grade.

No alarms sounded. No net dropped over her. The police weren't whipping out the handcuffs.

Quickly, Kieran stored the file. Then, unable to resist, she reopened it and there it was, a lovely B in her permanent record for last term.

Today, her school records. Tomorrow, the world. Just the way Hardball said it would be.

She raised her fist in salute and saw Amy passing the front window on her way back to the shop. Hastily, Kieran logged off and tried to look composed as Amy walked into the store.

"You have no idea how great it is to have someone we can trust so we can get some of our other business done," Amy said, bringing a bag of coins over to the register.

Kieran smiled. She told herself there was no reason to feel the little jab of guilt.

JON HAD BEEN GRANTED a momentary reprieve from kneading and rolling dough—his pop had decided it was time for him to learn the ropes out front.

"Working with the people," Demetri said, "this is the real test of the successful business."

Jon was ready for anything that didn't involve flour and yeast. Even a cash register.

"Bah!" Aurelia shook a finger at her brother-in-law. "You got no bread, you got no customers. They don't come in for your pretty face, Deme. See how long you last out here with nothing but that charm of yours."

"Don't listen to her," Demetri said, waving her off as he commandeered his son. "She thinks all you have to do is turn on the oven and the people show up, year after year. I tell you, it is how you treat them when they show up, this is the difference between success and failure.''

"And this boy, he's in such a mood to charm the customers," Aurelia said, her parting shot before she retreated to the back once again. "Never smiles. Smile and his face would crack, that's what."

Jon's frown deepened. She was right, of course. He wasn't sure if he'd had a cheerful word for anyone since coming home from Amy's two nights earlier. Not even for Kieran, who looked very different since starting work for Amy. She still treated Jon with surly indifference, but he told himself the physical changes were enough for the moment.

Demetri shrugged. "Never mind. You come."

Cash registers and customer service. No time for worrying about Amy. No time for trying to make sense out of the explosion of sensations and emotions that had come when he'd swept her up in that kiss.

Kiss was a tame description of what had happened between them.

Another few seconds and he would have been beyond mere kissing. Beyond stopping, even.

The worst of it was, he knew what had motivated him. Jealousy. Pure jealousy of that dapper-looking man who'd held Amy's attention at Java Joe's. But how to explain that kind of jealousy? How to explain what he'd felt when he kissed Amy?

The fulfilling of a lifelong fantasy, perhaps. That was plausible, it seemed to him. After all, he'd first started longing for Amy as an adolescent. A twenty-year buildup, that's what this was.

That explanation didn't satisfy him.

"So," Demetri said, "you get all that?"

"What?" Jon looked into his father's beaming face and realized he'd just missed lesson number one. *Sorry, Pop, I've been lusting after my ex-sister-in-law. Could you run that by me again?* "Yeah. Sure, Pop."

"Good, good. You help Mrs. Valentine and I will help the gentleman."

Jon looked toward the entrance, where a tall, lean man held the door open for Constance Valentine, who ran one of the bed-and-breakfast inns in town and came in daily for fresh baked goods.

"I'm afraid you now know my secret, Mr. Boyce," she was saying to the man Jon instantly recognized as the one he'd seen with Amy a few days earlier.

"Your secret is safe with me, Mrs. Valentine."

His voice was as smooth as his suit. Jon immediately wanted to warn Mrs. Valentine to keep her guard up. Ignoring his father's instructions, Jon walked up to the counter, looked the man straight in the eye and said, "What can I do for you?"

Mr. Boyce smiled at him, too, and said, all politeness, "Thank you, but I believe Mrs. Valentine was here first."

"Pop, you'll help Mrs. Valentine, won't you?"

Demetri shook his head and said, "Yes, sure. *I* help Mrs. Valentine. You do whatever you please."

Mr. Boyce's forehead creased slightly, as if he was trying to figure out the exchange that had just taken place between father and son, then smiled benignly. "All right, then. Could I have a loaf of your freshest bread?"

"It's all fresh this morning," Jon said, unable to dismiss the slight challenge in his voice. His father's foot came in his direction, clipping him on the ankle.

"I see. Very well, then. Whatever you recommend. Something special. A little gift, you see."

Jon was tempted to give him a loaf of the dark rye. Amy hated the dark rye. He told himself that was petty, beneath him.

What the hell. He did it anyway.

"You visiting Hurricane Beach?" he asked, trying for a friendly tone as he wrapped and rang up the bread.

"A little business," Mr. Boyce said. "A little pleasure."

Swell. Jon discovered he wasn't crazy about these feelings he had, especially when he had no alternative but to label them jealousy.

"Good. We hope you'll come back," he said, trying for the cordial tone his father always used with customers, and knowing he'd failed miserably. He didn't give a damn if Mr. Boyce with his thousand-dollar suit ever set foot in the Costas Family Bakery again.

Mr. Boyce called out a cheery goodbye to Mrs. Valentine and the bell jingled overhead to signal his departure.

"You wrap this for Mrs. Valentine," Demetri said sternly. "I go to the back for more cookies."

"Okay, Pop."

And as he passed, Demetri leaned close and whispered, "And be nice. Mrs. Valentine is a sweet lady. A regular."

Jon smiled at her, a much easier assignment than smiling at Mr. Boyce. "So, you know Mr. Boyce. Is he one of yours?"

Mrs. Valentine's smile brightened her face. "Yes, he is. He's been staying with me, oh, I'd say about three weeks now. A very nice man. And successful, too."

"Is he?"

"Oh, yes. His company, Silver Sands, I think, is the name of it, pays for everything. He must be very important. His given name is Palmer. I wonder if he's one of the Atlanta Palmers. On his mother's side, of course. The Atlanta Palmers were very important people, you know. I believe they once owned the Gresham cottage, if I'm not mistaken. I would ask him, but I hate to pry. Do you think it would be prying if I asked?"

He placed her package on the countertop and smiled. "Not at all, Mrs. Valentine. I'm sure he would welcome your interest."

Welcome or not, Jon decided as he rang up her

purchases and offered to have them delivered before lunch, he planned to do a little prying of his own. He'd call Bailey Bookman in New York that afternoon to ask for help in finding out what Palmer Boyce and Silver Sands were after in Hurricane Beach.

ON THE PHONE, his former colleague barely gave him time to get his request out before saying, "The office pool is laying odds that you'll be back before the six months is out. You gonna make me a winner, pal?"

Jon was surprised at the mixed feelings the question generated. He grappled for a noncommittal reply. "Didn't I say six months?"

"Sure, sure. But, listen, I've got something for you. Just in case you're getting ready to move on."

"What?"

"Remember Dexter Garland, the hotel guy?"

Jon smiled. Hotel guy was a totally inadequate title of the multimillionaire hotel magnate whose account Jon had handled. "Sure."

"He's got a proposition for you. Wanted me to put him in touch."

Jon felt a surge of excitement. "What kind of proposition?"

"You'll have to talk to him. He got real excited when I told him you were in Florida. I think he might have something cooking down there."

Jon took the number, telling his old friend he re-

ally wasn't interested yet, but it wouldn't hurt to
call. The truth was, Jon was more interested than he
wanted to say. More excited by the idea of getting
out of Hurricane Beach than he wanted to admit.

After all, wouldn't it be wise to get out of Dodge
before he really mucked things up?

"So," Bailey said, "why so curious about this
suit from Silver Sands?"

Jon hesitated. "My family's been doing business
here for forty years. I want to make sure nothing's
going to interfere with that."

The answer was plausible enough to satisfy his
old friend. But Jon knew the real reason was he
wanted to find out more about the character who'd
been hanging around Amy.

And that bugged Jon because he knew Palmer
Boyce probably had more right to hang around Amy
Hardaway than Jon did. Because Jon and Amy had
history. The kind of history that could get awfully
sticky.

Maybe it was past time to get out of Hurricane
Beach.

AMY WALKED down the beach from her parents'
house, oblivious to the rosy cast the setting sun gave
to the sand and water. Her sketch pad and drawing
supplies, untouched, were tucked into a canvas bag
slung over one shoulder. She had intended to lose
herself in her art this afternoon, but she'd been un-

able to find the lines, the shades, the picture in her head. She was too wrapped up in her worries.

She'd bypassed the gazebo completely, refusing even to look in its direction when she passed it.

Sam loped along at her side, pausing occasionally to sniff at a pile of seaweed or to yip at a sand crab scuttling to escape the dog's curiosity.

"If you loved me, you wouldn't be so cheerful," Amy grumbled to the dog.

Sam responded by chasing the seafoam as it receded to meet the next wave. He looked at her with a happy smile when the foam got away from him.

"Mutt." She used the word as endearment. Sam galloped back to her side and allowed her to rub the top of his head. "You have no idea my life is falling apart around me, do you?"

After struggling to draw for forty-five minutes, Amy had decided to give up and visit her parents. When she arrived at Sea Haven, Merrick had been gone. Helene had been sitting on the deck alone, staring out over the gulf, the ice melting in her untouched lemonade.

"Where's Dad?" Amy asked.

"Walking." Helene sounded listless and small.

"Alone?" Amy immediately wanted to take back the word, Helene looked so forlorn.

"We...your father finds walking alone more restful lately."

Amy sat on the floor, Sam at her side, looking up at her mother. She still felt torn between confronting her parents with what she had learned from Palmer Boyce, or calling her sisters first. Looking at her mother, hearing the defeat in her voice, Amy knew she wasn't up to dealing with this alone.

Instead, she had spent the next hour talking to her mother about trivialities, hoping to distract her. They talked about the shop, about the lengthening days and the rising humidity, about how Grace was coping with her recent heartbreak. Which led to the other topic that didn't feel so trivial for Amy at the moment.

"Have you run into Jon since he came home?" Helene asked.

"Yes." Amy strove for a casual tone. She remembered the way he'd kissed her. She could still feel it if she closed her eyes. Or even if she didn't, as she'd learned when she tried to draw this afternoon. "Yes, I see him…often."

*Too often.*

*Not often enough.*

"I hear he's gone completely gray."

Her mother's words didn't do justice to the gleaming silver of Jon's short, crisp hair. She wondered, suddenly, how those silver threads would feel in her fingers. Told herself she'd never know.

God help her, surely she would never know.

"Yes," she said. It was all she could manage.

"He must look dreadful."

Amy almost choked on her reply. "No. Actually, he wears it well."

"Lisa should never have left him."

A sentiment Amy had heard many times. One she had agreed with. But did she still? "I know."

"I sometimes think she hasn't had a happy moment since."

Amy's spirits sank even lower. She imagined, for a moment, what her mother would say if she'd come upon Amy and her ex-brother-in-law the night he kissed her. The notion was too grim to consider for more than a second. "I know."

"I must admit," Helene continued, "when I heard he was home, I couldn't help but think that...perhaps the next time Lisa comes home... Well, you never know."

The visit with her mother had done nothing to improve Amy's mood. On the contrary, she left Sea Haven with her emotions a scramble of fear and guilt and sadness. The chances of mending things with Lisa were slipping away. And she had no one to blame but herself.

"What happens if Lisa shows up for Spring Break?" she said to Sam as they trudged toward home.

Sam gave an encouraging yip.

Amy created scenario after scenario in her head, trying to envision some harmless way for this situation to play itself out. None of them could be classified a happy ending.

There was the one where Lisa ended up brokenhearted. The one where Lisa ended up angry and vowing never to speak to her sister again. And one of Amy's personal favorites, the one where everyone else in the family ostracized her, as well, including her parents and Megan. The only consolation in that particular scenario was that the scandal brought her parents back together.

Small consolation. Very small.

Then there was the scenario where Jon and Lisa spotted each other across a crowded room and realized they'd been fools to ever let one another go. They lived happily ever after. The families were ecstatic. Nick even quit drugs forever and Kieran got a scholarship to Harvard, thanks to the shining beacon of Lisa and Jon's love.

That was the one that hurt Amy the most. But it was also the only one that hurt nobody else.

"Come on, Sam," she said as she turned up the beach toward her house. "Let's watch comedy videos. Every single comedy act we've taped. We'll have an orgy of comedy."

She topped the dune and saw Jon Costas sitting on the top step to her deck. He smiled when he saw her, and stood. Amy's heart stopped when he smiled. Her step faltered as she tried to figure out if there was any plausible way to get away from him without turning and running like a coward.

Nothing came to mind.

"What are you doing here?"

His thousand-watt smile dimmed perceptibly. Just enough to enable Amy to get her feet moving again.

She stood on her bottom step and looked up at him. A flash of heat spread through her. She remembered the feel of his body, long and hard against hers.

She had to sit down before her knees gave way. But he was blocking her path.

He took two steps down, reached for her hand and led her up the steps. His flesh felt cool against hers. Of course, hers was overheated.

"Come on," he said. "We're gonna have some fireworks tonight."

## CHAPTER TEN

JON KNEW he was behaving like a desperate man. His judgment had fled, all rational behavior had abandoned him. He'd dissected this situation to kingdom come and it hadn't helped.

Oh, boy.

"What are you talking about?" That breathy voice of hers wrapped itself around him.

*Keep focused,* he told himself. *Don't do anything she'll want to kick you out for.*

He slipped the video out of the pocket of his windbreaker and waved it. "Fireworks. I've been talking to a company in Valdosta and they sent me a video of some of their best stuff. Consider it an audition for the Spring Break fireworks display."

He pulled her toward the house, discovered the door was unlocked.

"Jon, I don't need to see this," she said, allowing him to pull her into the living room. "If you want to use this company in Valdosta, do it. It's okay with me."

He shook his head, took the canvas bag from her shoulder and put his hands on her shoulders, pushing her onto a love seat. "No, no, no. You're the committee. We'll need a vote. This ought to be official."

"Consider it official. I'll do whatever you want."

Jon decided to ignore that comment and concentrate on which buttons to push to get her VCR operating. He heard whirs and clicks. He walked back to the love seat. Sam had already joined her.

"Sorry, Fido." He urged the dog to the floor.

"His name is Sam. And he's fine where he is."

"No, this is my seat. Sam's getting the popcorn." She prepared to get up. "Jon, I—"

"Shh. It's starting." He took her hand and held it firmly. "I hate missing the opening credits, don't you? And previews of coming attractions. What if they have previews?"

"They won't have previews. Jon—"

"Look! Look!" He gestured toward the TV. "This is what they did last year in Montgomery. For Independence Day. Now, watch. This is a big decision."

With a heavy sigh, she grew still beside him.

For the next twenty minutes, the only fireworks Jon was aware of were the ones going on within him. And they were spectacular.

KIERAN'S BEDROOM was lit only by the eerie glow of her computer screen. The only sound in the room was the *tap-tap-tap* of her fingers on the keys.

TO: Hardball
FROM: Beach Bunny
Gonzo news. The shop is linked to all kinds of stuff—the library, the schools and—TA-DA!—the bank. Tell me what to do.

She waited, cruising the other bulletin boards for interesting chat. On the adults-only line, tonight's chat was about multiple orgasm. She checked her mailbox again.

TO: Beach Bunny
FROM: Hardball
So, my little Beach Bunny wants to be a Money Bunny! Say, if you play this right, we could start our own little travel fund right now. I could come visit. What do you say to a little F2F?

Kieran's heart lurched happily. F2F. Face-to-face. She stood up and did a crazy pirouette around the room. Hardball wanted to meet her!

"Yes!" She sat back down and scrolled through the rest of his message.

Here's all you do to set up an account using money transferred from other accounts—your sweet uncle Jon's bakery, for example, or even the store where you work. We'll be rich in no time.

The part about taking money from Rêve Rags bothered Kieran a little. Amy—and even Grace—had been so terrific. They didn't treat her like a kid at all. She really didn't want to do anything to hurt them. But Hardball was right about one thing. The family owed her. For the way her old man had dumped her, for the way they never understood her, for the way they tried to bully her around.

For the way none of them wanted to be there for her.

That's all you have to do, Bunny. If you have any questions, you know where to find me. Otherwise, I'll be planning my itinerary and dreaming of your sweet face.

Kieran closed out her mailbox and started on a long reply, telling her friend how eager she was to see him. She described the abandoned shack on the pier five miles down the coast, where they could go to be alone. She hugged herself, feeling delirious with anticipation, and tapped the key that would ship her message straight to Hardball's private electronic mailbox.

Face-to-face. She couldn't wait.

THE FIREWORKS on her TV screen were nothing compared to the fireworks going on inside Amy.

She didn't dare look at Jon. Didn't dare move for fear of touching him, brushing against him. He still held her hand, but she had willed herself to forget that. And she had scooted to the edge of the love seat, where she stiffened herself against any other physical contact.

It hardly mattered. His nearness seemed to be all her body needed to set it off.

Her breathing was shallow because her chest felt tight, her throat closed. By the time the video ended, she was light-headed.

They watched the blank screen for several moments before Jon said, "So, what do you think?"

His voice sounded strange. And that alarmed Amy. It was hard enough feeling off-center herself; it didn't help a bit to think Jon might be feeling the same way.

She cleared her throat. "Fine. Good."

She slipped her hand out of his.

"Good? I don't want good."

"No?"

"I want...stupendous. I want to...light up the sky like it's never been done before."

His voice drew her to meet his gaze and she couldn't resist the lure any longer. His eyes were as intense as she had feared they would be. And they were focused entirely on her. Amy's heart fluttered with a nervous certainty that he was talking about much more than a few colorful explosions set off to get people in a festive mood.

"Yes," she said. "You can do that, I think."

"We," he said. "We're a team, remember?"

What she remembered was the soft insistence of his lips on hers. She leaped off the love seat, startling Sam, who opened a disapproving eye. She snatched the remote control and began rewinding the video.

"Remember that first Spring Break after you and Lisa got married?"

He frowned and she took that for an answer.

"The fireworks were good that year, don't you think?"

"I really don't remember," he said.

"Oh, they were." For all she knew, there hadn't been any fireworks that year. The thing she remembered best from that time was how hard it had been to keep her thoughts off Jon.

At least then, she'd had young and foolish to blame it on. *And what's your excuse now?*

"But these will be better," she prattled, retrieving the video, slipping it into its box and thrusting it toward Jon. "No question. Let's book them. Right away."

He ignored the video, staring at her face instead. Amy felt her cheeks grow warm. He could see right through her silly behavior. This wasn't working. She dropped the video into his lap.

"You should go."

"Why?"

She gave up the pretense. "You know why."

"Tell me."

"Because I don't want you to kiss me again."

He grinned. Darn his hide, he grinned! "Don't you?"

"No!"

She wheeled and paced the room, arms wrapped tightly around her chest. When she faced him once more, he was standing at the window beside the door onto the deck, slapping the video against his palm.

"We ought to quit pretending," he said.

"I don't want to talk about it."

"I know what I feel." With his eyes and his tone, he challenged her to admit the truth, as well.

"This is impossible. You know that, don't you?"

"Why?"

"*Why?* You were married to my sister. You haven't forgotten that, have you?"

"That was a long time ago."

"I'm not sure there's a statute of limitations on getting involved with your sister's ex."

He shoved the video into his jacket pocket. He looked disgruntled.

*Good.*

"Amy, it's not like I'm proposing ma—"

"Don't even say it."

"It's not going to go away, you know."

"Yes, it will. I'll stay out of your way. You stay out of mine. It's always worked before."

"What's that mean?"

Amy sucked in her breath, knowing she'd said too much. "Nothing. Now, go away. Before we do something we can't take back."

His grin was softer, tempered. "Too late for that."

And he might as well have been kissing her right then, for his words swept everything she'd wanted to avoid talking about into the room with them. The way he'd kissed her, touched her, and the way she'd wanted him. Deeply. Desperately.

The image washed through her, prickling her flesh, leaving her weak.

"What about Lisa?" she asked.

"That was a long time ago, Amy. I don't love your sister and she doesn't love me."

Shows what he knew. "How can you be sure of that?"

"I know my own mind."

She studied his face for any hint that he was fooling himself. "Really?"

"Look, Lisa and I were a mistake from the beginning. We were too young. We were—I was looking for someone to make me feel good about myself. It doesn't work that way."

"It doesn't?" Of course it did. What did he know? She thought of what her mother had said, that Lisa hadn't seemed happy since she and Jon split up.

He shook his head.

"But Lisa—"

"Lisa kicked me out. Not that I blame her. I was self-absorbed and immature. I was no Prince Charming."

"Jon, all that matters is that the past is real and we can't ignore it."

Pursing his lips, he studied her and she longed, as she so often did, for the ability to see behind those baffling eyes of his. Then he surprised her, reaching out and brushing his fingers along her jawline.

"I've always wanted you, you know."

Her heart turned over in her chest. She closed her eyes, as if that might help her avoid hearing what her soul so desperately wanted to hear. "That's not so."

"Yes, it is. Sometimes I think it was always you."

She withdrew from his touch and turned away, unable to look at him for fear he would read the truth in her face. "Don't go there, Jon."

He turned and walked to the door, looking back only long enough to repeat, "This isn't going away, Amy. This is what's real today, and it has nothing to do with what happened between Lisa and me years ago. So let me know when you're ready to live in today."

She stood rooted to the spot when he left, knowing only that she had to be grateful he'd gone. For if he hadn't, she knew what was destined to happen between them.

In turmoil, she paced her cottage for the next hour, the dilemmas in her life twisting round and round in her head. What to do about her sisters. And her parents. About the offer from Silver Sands. And

Jon, of course, and her own out-of-control emotions. Her life had never been such a mess. Never.

She dialed Grace, but the line was busy.

Fifteen minutes later, still busy. And fifteen minutes after that. That meant Grace was probably on long distance to her family in Mississippi, a weekly phone orgy that would boost telephone-company stock through the ceiling by the following morning.

Sam moaned, urging her to settle down. She was probably getting on his nerves.

"Okay," she said. "Megan. I'll tell Megan about the Silver Sands offer. That much, at least, we can decide how to handle."

She punched in her older sister's number and waited for the ring. But it wasn't Megan's voice that answered. It was Lisa's. Amy covered her mouth. How could she have made a mistake like that.

A cosmic message from the universe, she decided. A dose of guilt from the angel of serendipity.

"Who is this?" Lisa's impatient voice prodded her.

"Oh. Sorry. It's me. Amy."

"What's wrong, Amy?"

*What's wrong? Nothing. I've been throwing myself at your ex-husband, but don't worry, I'm ready to back off. He's saying crazy things, that he wanted me all along. But I know better than that. Even Mom agrees, the two of you need each other. What's wrong? How could anything be wrong?*

"I, um, it's about Mom and Dad."

"Tell me, Amy."

*Yes. Tell her about the kiss. About the way you felt when he held your hand.*

"They're thinking about selling the property. Well, actually, Dad's thinking about selling it. Mom doesn't want to."

"Selling Sea Haven?"

Amy filled her sister in on all the details, about Palmer Boyce and the Silver Sands Development Company and how the offer was tearing their parents apart and the pressure that Boyce had put on her to help them decide.

"And I don't know what to do," she finished. "I don't know what's right. I...so I decided to call. For help."

"How much did you say this company is offering?"

Amy repeated the offer. "But he said they might go higher."

In the brief silence that followed, Amy tried to imagine Lisa's face. The only face that came to her was Jon's.

Lisa said, "Have you talked to Megan about this?"

"Not yet."

"But she's coming for Spring Break?"

"That's right."

"I'll be there, too."

As she hung up a few minutes later, Amy didn't

know whether or not to be glad that her sister had decided to come.

How in the world could she face Lisa?

## CHAPTER ELEVEN

AMY WOULDN'T have been at the gazebo in the first place if the little girls from her art class at the Y hadn't been so insistent.

"Please, please, please!" Jodi had said, her soulful brown eyes wider than usual. Six-year-old Jodi already knew where her greatest talent lay.

So they were at the gazebo, painting seascapes, when Jon found them.

Sitting in a noisy circle were six little girls, ages four to six, wearing oversize shirts Amy had supplied. The large rectangles of paper in front of them were smeared with watercolors. So were their arms, their faces and Amy's shirts. The class, as always, was an exercise in patience. Amy had to show Rashia once again which colors mixed together to create green. She had to give the seal of approval to Jana Marie's rendition of a sea gull. She had to wipe up spills and give the girls ideas on improving their technique in ways that preschoolers could understand.

Amy loved her class. But right now, she didn't love being at the gazebo. She didn't need the reminders.

Then he appeared on the beach, all broad shoulders and sun-bronzed skin and hair glinting silver in the midday sun. And she knew it was no coincidence.

Their gazes locked as he approached. Hers, she supposed, were full of the way she'd been missing him the past few days when neither of them had had the courage to search the other out. His, as always, were unreadable.

"I've been thinking," he said without preamble.

She thought of telling him she didn't want to know what he'd been thinking. But that would have been a lie. She wanted to know. Desperately.

"Miss Amy!" A high-pitched voice broke through the tension. "Miss Amy, Cammi spilled the water!"

Six little girls began to squeal and giggle. Amy retrieved a jumbo roll of paper towels and mopped up the water, refereeing the debate over who had caused the disaster.

When she finished cleaning the mess, Jon was still there. Amy became aware of the heavy thump of her heart, and of the heat seeping through her body.

"I've been thinking," he repeated. He fidgeted with his watch. "You're probably right. About—" he looked toward the little girls and lowered his voice "—about us."

A little part of Amy died, like a flicker of light going out. It was the first hint she'd had that she'd been holding on to hope, that a dream or two were still alive.

"Things are too complicated, with Lisa and our families, all that history."

She told herself to smile, to nod, to let him see that she still agreed. But she couldn't. Not yet.

"We need to concentrate on being friends," he continued. "You know, keep it platonic. There's no reason we can't do that. Is there?"

The voice that replied sounded faraway to her, a little unreal. "Of course not. That's...that's all I've ever wanted."

"Miss Amy! Miss Amy, Emily got pink on my blue fish!"

"In a minute, Cammi."

Jon began to approach her, edging nearer along the railing. "Good."

Except that Amy couldn't think of a thing to say to him, friend to friend. She was no longer interested in painting a glowing portrait of her sister, even though a part of her still said that was the right thing to do. When Cammi called her again, she shrugged apologetically and went to mediate another dispute.

Maybe he would leave.

She hoped so. Didn't she?

Jon stayed. Now Amy glanced at her watch. Another half hour and she could excuse herself, start helping the girls pack up.

"You're good with the kids," he said after a while.

"I like teaching them. When they're this little, they don't have any inhibitions."

He nodded and looked as if he wanted to say more. The silence grew heavy between them.

"You're a good teacher. And a good artist. I'll bet you did the mural at your shop, too." Jon's smile softened both the stiffness in his face and the tension gripping Amy. Of course, she thought, after all that's happened, it would take a little time to get comfortable with each other again. But it could work. She relaxed her shoulders.

Anything seemed possible in the sunshine of Jon's smile.

"Thanks."

Then he just kept asking questions about her art and she kept answering them and soon all the tension seemed to have dissipated. When it came time to pack up her class, Amy realized that she was smiling at Jon, and it made her feel warm clear through.

Friends. It was certainly a good idea.

Jon helped gather the painting supplies and occupied the girls with silly questions. He was good with kids, too, she noticed. The end of the class went smoother than usual. No one pouted and whined about not being finished. Everyone was eager to show Jon her painting and receive the blessing of his captivating smile.

No age was immune to that smile, apparently.

They followed the little girls down the beach.

Amy felt so companionable she almost linked her arm through his.

Friends could do that, couldn't they?

THE NEXT COUPLE OF WEEKS were a frenzy of activity, for which Amy was grateful. The frantic pace made it easier to ignore the forlorn little voice in her head that said she didn't want to be Jon Costas's friend.

But she was too busy to obsess, too busy to be anything but grateful that she and Jon could finally be realistic and work on being friends.

And they *were* working on it. One of the things keeping Amy busy was final plans for Spring Break festivities. The merchants' association met twice in one week. Jon and Amy talked almost every day, hashing out details for the fireworks display, reminding each other of things they couldn't afford to forget.

"I'm glad we cleared the air," she said to him one evening as they sat on the pier to judge the exact time of sunset, to make sure they'd chosen the right time for starting the fireworks. After all, the *Almanac* could be wrong by a few minutes in either direction. Right?

"Me, too," he said.

His voice was soft, as soft as the early twilight enveloping them.

See how well things were going, she told herself, that she could sit here beside him and elicit virtually no physical response from him. He hadn't touched her, hadn't looked deeply into her eyes, nothing out of the way, despite all the time they were spending together.

She sighed. "I guess our timing was right all along. On the fireworks, I mean."

Actually, their timing was right on this friendship business, too. They were getting a little better at it each day. In time, Amy thought, they would have it down pat.

By the time Lisa got to town, for example.

Thank goodness she was too busy to think about Jon in any other way. For one thing, there was Palmer Boyce. The Silver Sands representative constantly applied subtle pressure on her to talk her parents into selling Sea Haven. He showed up at the shop more than once to chat, looking so suave and acting so ingratiatingly that neither Kieran nor Grace could stomach him.

"Watch out for him, Amy," Grace said. "He's too slick."

"That means he's a sleaze," Kieran clarified. "You're not, like, *dating* him, are you?"

"Of course not."

They'd just finished inventory. One of the many other things that had kept her too busy to think about Jon. Amy and Grace and Kieran had worked hard to get Rêve Rags in tip-top shape for the extra business Spring Break would bring. They cleaned. They racked new merchandise. They nitpicked their displays until every item in the store looked picture-perfect.

"You really like it?" Kieran asked, looking around at the newly reorganized store.

The teen had suggested color-grouped racks instead of racks organized by size. The new displays created bursts of brightness throughout the shop, a rainbow of eye appeal that made it easier for customers to coordinate clothes and accessories. Everyone commented how much they liked the new arrangement and how much more fun it made shopping. Kieran's suggestion was a hit.

Amy smiled and put an arm around the uncertain girl's shoulders. "I don't like it. I love it. It's terrific. So terrific I'm going to buy you pizza for dinner."

"Cool."

They bought a medium pizza—half vegetarian, half Italian sausage and pepperoni—at the back window of Slice of the Pie and sat on the pier, legs dangling over the edge, facing the lowering sun.

"You ever think about leaving Hurricane Beach?" Kieran said.

"Sure." Amy gestured down the beach. "About five or six miles in that direction, there's an old pier with a little shack on it. That's where I used to go whenever I felt rotten. It's been abandoned so long, I doubt if it's even there anymore."

"It's there," Kieran said.

"Is it?"

"Yeah. I went there. Once." Kieran bent her

straw and studied it carefully. "You don't ever want to get away like that now?"

Amy shook her head. "No. But when I was your age, that's where I'd go. I'd walk out to the edge of the pier and look all around and imagine what it would be like to get as far away from there as I could go."

"Yeah?"

"Yeah. But when I finished college, I don't know, it just felt right to come home."

Kieran frowned skeptically and Amy knew exactly what her young friend was thinking. She couldn't have imagined herself feeling that way, either, at fifteen. And she'd had none of the problems Kieran had. But for once, her compulsion to fix other people's lives didn't come to the fore. She'd decided that simply being available and nonjudgmental might be the best way to get Kieran to open up.

Or at least to teach her that sometimes grown-ups can be trusted.

And miracle of miracles, her approach seemed to be working. It had begun to occur to Amy that the only life she'd really had a hand in changing was Kieran's. And it had happened the only time in her life she'd simply let go and allowed things to take their natural course.

So much for her license to fix everything.

Kieran crushed the pizza box, and said, "It's worse now, you know. At home, I mean."

"Why?"

The girl frowned. "Because of Uncle Jon. He can't wait to get out of this place and he takes it out on me because he thinks if I keep lousing up he'll never get to go back to the real world."

Amy felt a tug of identification. She wasn't the only one who didn't have the power to make Jon Costas want to stay in Hurricane Beach. But her own problems, she knew, were petty next to Kieran's. "So he's kind of hard on you, huh?"

"Yeah."

"That's tough. Especially when you're not used to having somebody look over your shoulder."

"That's why I like working for you and Grace. Because you're not always nagging me."

"Of course not. We trust you."

Kieran startled her then by jumping up unexpectedly, shoving the pizza box into the trash barrel and saying, "Gotta run."

Amy watched her dart back toward Gulfview, wondering what had prompted Kieran's hasty retreat.

THE MEETING with the Panama City radio station that was to simulcast an all-patriotic music selection to coincide with the Spring Break fireworks went well. Now it was time for Amy and Jon to get into his pop's station wagon and drive back to Hurricane Beach.

"We'll be home in time for dinner," Jon said,

jiggling the keys in his pocket and wishing there were some way to prolong this time with Amy. "We don't dress for dinner anymore, we put on combat fatigues."

Amy looked into his eyes over the top of the car and he wondered what had possessed him to tell this woman they could just be friends. He was lost, lost, lost, and he'd been out of his mind to think he could forget the way he felt about her.

She grinned at him, that impish grin that made him want to sweep her into his arms and whirl her around until they were both dizzy. At which point they would fall into a heap on the beach and...

*Oh, damn.*

"We could ride the Tilt-a-whirl instead," she said, her green eyes lighting up.

"The Tilt-a-whirl?"

She nodded toward the small amusement park across the street, a garish open-air park full of rides and games, adorned with enough neon to give Times Square some serious competition.

"Right over there," she said, closing her car door and walking around the hood to take him by the hand, "they have a Ferris wheel and a carousel and a ringtoss game."

"Ringtoss?"

He was already walking toward the corner with her, hypnotized by her long fingers intertwined through his, and by the delight in her sparkling eyes.

"I won the giant teddy bear—a green one—in 1977," she said.

"Old glories don't count," he said after they sprinted across the busy street.

"I can beat *your* pants off."

Hoping she didn't notice his wince, he dropped her hand and dug in his pockets for change. "Not a prayer."

They rode the Tilt-a-whirl, which sent them spinning from one side of the curved car to the other, crushed to each other's sides, leaving Amy breathless from laughing and Jon breathless from her nearness. They rode the Ferris wheel, which Amy insisted on rocking recklessly when it paused at the top. They played ringtoss and she won a very ugly Kewpie doll, which she presented to him.

"And still champion," he said. "I'll buy you a snow cone."

"Make it cotton candy and I'll consider myself justly rewarded."

A few minutes later, cotton candy and snow cone in hand, they wandered through the arcade.

"I haven't been in one of these places in years," Jon said. "Decades, maybe."

Amy frowned and licked pink sugar off the tips of her fingers. "You've been too grown-up."

"Isn't that what we're supposed to do?" he said. "Grow up, become responsible?"

"I don't think so. I never saw that in the instruction manual. Did you?"

"The instruction manual?"

"For life. Didn't you get yours?"

He shrugged and smiled. "Loan me yours?"

"I don't know," she said. "Maybe mine has secrets you're not supposed to know. Girl secrets."

"That hardly seems like a fair way to run the universe."

"Fair? You wanted fair? If you'd had the manual, you would've known better than that."

They bantered away as much of the afternoon as Jon could justify. Every time Amy mentioned leaving, he would coax her into one more round of video race cars or one more bag of peanuts. Finally, he could delay no longer and they headed down the coastal highway toward home. Amy slouched down in the passenger seat, a bare arm hanging out the open window. The breeze ruffled her hair. Her eyes were closed and her still-pink lips were smiling faintly.

Jon wondered if her lips tasted of cotton candy. He felt relaxed and happy, and thought of how often he felt that way around Amy.

And that made him think of Palmer Boyce and what his friend in New York had told him earlier in the day.

"I know about the Silver Sands offer," he said.

Her eyes snapped open. "How did you find out?"

He didn't want to tell her he'd checked up on Palmer Boyce. *Oh, by the way, I'm only interested in being friends, myself, but I'm damn sure jealous of this Boyce character.* "It's a small town."

"Who else knows?"

"Nobody, yet."

Her arm crept back into the car. The hint of a smile had vanished. "But that won't be the case for long."

"Will Helene and Merrick sell?"

She sighed. "Who knows."

"Is this why they aren't getting along?"

"Who else is aware of that?"

"Everybody."

"Oh, man." She slipped her feet into her sandals and sat up straight. "Boyce wants me to convince them to sell."

He thought of her parents selling all that prime beachfront property. But his first thought wasn't of what the sale would do to Hurricane Beach. His first thought was what Amy would do if her parents left.

What if she left, too? He had a moment of panic, imagining Hurricane Beach without Amy, until he remembered that he wouldn't be around himself. What difference would it make what Amy did?

Still, the thought disturbed him.

"Are you going to?"

"I don't know. I don't know what to do. We're going to discuss it at Spring Break." Was it his imagination, or did she press herself a little closer to the passenger door? "Megan and Lisa and me."

He was silent, wondering how he and Lisa would

react to each other. Especially given the way he felt about Amy. Would Lisa be able to see it in his face? Would she warn Amy against him?

As if Amy needed warning. She'd decided all on her own that Jon Costas was bad news in her life.

Big surprise that should be. He was her sister's ex-husband. God knows what Lisa had said about him. Would say about him again when she realized he and Amy were friends.

Friends. What a joke.

Lisa wouldn't be laughing.

"I guess you look forward to seeing her," Amy said.

No right answers to that one, Jon knew. A no would make him sound like one of those bitter ex-spouses who held grudges. A yes would make him sound like a man still pining for the love of his life.

"Well, yes and no." It seemed like a clever out, until he spoke the words. Once he heard them out loud, it simply sounded as if he'd double damned himself.

"What does that mean?"

"It means...well, I haven't seen her in a long time. So it will be nice to see her. On the other hand, I haven't seen her in such a long time that...well, seeing her won't be easy."

"I see," Amy said.

"It's confusing," he said.

"Obviously."

The rest of the ride home was spent in silence.

KIERAN HELD her breath as the bank teller punched keys on her computer. Would they find her out now?

A part of her almost hoped they would. As soon as Amy said she trusted her, guilt had all but overwhelmed Kieran. They trusted her. And she was stealing money. Using their shop, their computer, she was committing fraud, and the FBI had probably already figured it out and this teller had probably stepped on the alarm under her station and the police were probably on the way and they would haul her off in handcuffs.

She looked down at the little blue sweater tied around her waist—the one Amy had insisted she take when it came into the store because it matched the skirt Amy had given her the week before—and wondered if she could use it to cover her head when they took her out. So the camera crews couldn't put her on TV. She'd seen that before.

"And you say you don't have your passbook with you?" the teller said.

Kieran jumped. "Um, no. Not with me."

The young woman smiled. "Do you have some ID?"

Kieran swallowed hard. What would happen, she wondered, if she just turned and ran. Right now? Would they chase her? Where could she go? And how would she ever get in touch with Hardball again? With fingers that trembled, she pulled out her picture ID from school and pushed it across the counter.

Interminable minutes later, the young woman pushed the ID card and another slip of paper across the counter. "Your balance. Will there be anything else?"

Kieran snatched the card and the paper, mumbled a reply and got out of the bank as quickly as her legs would carry her. Even when she reached the beach, she didn't slow down. Heart bursting with anxiety, she ran all the way to the pier. Ignoring the No Trespassing sign, she made her way through the rusty opening in the chain-link fence and waded into the shallow water. She climbed the rickety old ladder to the pier.

There, huddled against the damp wall of the little shack, she dropped to her knees and unfolded the crumpled paper still clutched in her fist. When she saw the amount written there, she began to smile.

It was working.

She counted up how many days it would be before she saw Hardball.

JON HAD MADE UP his mind. This friendship business was for the birds.

Armed with a bag of fresh *kourabiedes* and baklava—he'd made the phyllo himself, a feat that had pleased and astonished Aurelia—he walked to Amy's beach house, determined to tell her. That way, things would be out in the open when Lisa arrived.

She was in the hammock, feet in the air, eyes closed, her loose white pants riding up to her knees.

The steps creaked on his way up. Sam woofed softly. Amy opened one eye. "Well, hi."

She sounded pleased to see him. His heart grew a little lighter.

"I brought you some goodies," he said. "Cookies. And baklava, made with my first phyllo."

She took the bag without rising and gestured toward the deck chair facing the beach. He turned it toward her and sat.

"I'm honored," she said.

"You should be." He smiled and was rewarded when she returned the smile. "I have it on good authority that baking is an art form."

"Come on, Sam," she said, peeking into the bag, then reaching in to pinch a corner of one of the honey-drenched, diamond-shaped pastries. "He's my official taster. If Sam doesn't turn his nose up at it, it's safe to eat."

Sam didn't turn his nose up at it. In fact, the dog mooched about half the pastry while Amy enjoyed the rest of it. Jon simply enjoyed watching her eat it, licking honey off her fingers.

Now. Tell her now. That you made a mistake. That you don't want to be her friend. That what you want is... That the way you feel is... "Amy, I've been thinking."

"Okay. Shoot."

She wiped her fingers on the napkins he'd stuck in the bag.

"About what I said the other day," he told her. "About being friends."

A wary look crossed her face and Jon felt fear in his heart. Things had been going well. He got to see her. Joke with her. What if she pitched him off her deck? Told him not to come back? And she might, if he told her how he really felt.

*And how is that?*

"I thought it was working out," Amy said.

"Oh, it is," he said hastily. "Except…"

"Except what?"

*Except that I love you too much to be your friend.*

For one heart-stopping moment, Jon feared he'd spoken the words aloud. Then he realized that Amy still looked at him questioningly. She hadn't sicced Sam on him or thrown his bag of pastries in his face.

Besides, that wasn't what he'd intended to say at all. What he'd intended to say was, well, something about how much stronger his feelings were than simple friendship. And how much he wanted her. That's right. Don't forget wanting her. Focus on wanting her.

*Why? So I won't have to think about loving her?*

"What is it, Jon?"

His heart slammed against his ribs. "Nothing," he said. "Just that I hope things won't change just because…of Lisa. When she comes home, I mean."

He realized he'd begun to perspire. But at least

he'd managed to get something out without straying into territory so dangerous even he didn't have a clue how to maneuver through it.

"Oh," she said. "Lisa."

"Because I'll still feel the same way—that friendly way, I mean. No matter what happens with Lisa."

Did that come out right? From the look on Amy's face, he doubted it.

"I understand, Jon. And I won't feel any differently, either. I promise."

Jon escaped quickly after that and pondered his close call all the way home. Given the unexpected emergence of the L word, he seemed to have only one choice. Maybe it was time to call Dexter Garland, the hotel magnate, and plan his escape route.

HELENE FROZE, and put her hand against the side of her daughter's house to steady herself.

She'd had no intention of eavesdropping, of course. She'd simply parked at the front of Amy's and when her knocks drew no response at the front door, she'd walked around to see if Amy was on her deck.

She stood there willing her rapid heartbeat to subside, trying to decide whether she could sneak off without giving herself away. Because she wasn't prepared to talk to Amy about this yet. What she'd overheard had startled her entirely too much to discuss it with her daughter.

Amy and Jon. She shook her head. There was no denying the subtext of the conversation between the two of them. They could talk about being friends all day long, but Helene knew what she'd heard.

She would have to tell Merrick, of course. Merrick would know what to do.

Of course, Merrick might want to punch that young man in the nose. Helene smiled. Yes, he might want to do just that.

And that, of course, might make it impossible for them to get through the girls' upcoming visit without this situation coming out in the open. If her daughters were alienated now, what would this do to them?

Oh, dear. And just when she thought things couldn't possibly get any more complicated.

# CHAPTER TWELVE

BANK STATEMENT clutched in her fist, Amy headed down Gulfview toward the bank.

Jon Costas caught her eye.

He was standing in the doorway of the bakery, lounging against the frame talking to Maida from the art gallery. His apron was tied at the front and immaculately white against his bronzed skin. He reminded Amy of times long past, a bit old-fashioned, but solid and dependable. Amy smiled, wondering how the wheeler-dealer in him would like being viewed as old-fashioned and dependable. Then he smiled at Maida and her little dog and Amy forgot all about the discrepancy in Rêve Rags' account.

Her heart breathed his name.

By the time she managed to convince herself to get on with her visit to the bank to figure out where two hundred dollars from last week's receipts had vanished, Jon was waving goodbye to Maida. He spotted Amy and his hand froze in midair, the same way Amy had frozen.

*Jon.*

She shook herself, broke the spell. She waved and smiled and decided the bank could wait five minutes. She walked toward Jon. He glanced over his shoulder, into the bakery, then met her in front of the florist's.

"You've got time for lounging in the doorway, I see," she said, smiling because he made her feel like smiling, and talking because it helped cover the sound of his name as it rushed through her. "Your mom's back must be better today."

"Not much. She bends all wrong. I keep trying to tell her, but she won't listen."

She took a step in the direction of the bakery. "I think I'll go tell her about an exercise I learned in yoga class. What you do is—"

Jon stepped in front of her. "Um...you don't have to do that. You're on your way to the bank, aren't you?" he asked, looking at the ledger she was carrying.

"It'll only take a minute."

"Nothing takes a minute with my family. You go in there and you'll have to demonstrate, then Thea Aurelia will want a blow-by-blow history of how you learned the exercise. 'What, a girl your age with back trouble? What's wrong with you American girls?'"

Amy grinned. He was right, of course. "'So? The bank is going somewhere this afternoon?'" She did her best Aurelia impression and took another step.

Again, he angled in front of her. "It's...we're pretty busy in the kitchen right now. Maybe another time would be better."

"Funny. *You* don't look all that busy."

What he looked was distinctly uncomfortable. He'd tried holding on to his smile, but it vanished completely now. "Aw, Amy—"

"What is it, Jon?"

He shoved his hands deep into the pockets of his faded khakis and looked at his feet.

"What's wrong?"

"Nothing's *wrong,* exactly."

She walked around him and he let her go. When she got to the window of the bakery, she saw what he hadn't wanted her to see. Her mother sat at one of the little tables with Palmer Boyce. She was laughing, something Amy had seen darn little of from Helene Hardaway lately. And in her eyes was that coy expression Amy recognized as flirtation.

Anger flashed through Amy and she took another step toward the door, until she felt a restraining hand on her arm.

"Let me go!" she snapped, whirling to face Jon.

He didn't release her. "Leave it alone, Amy. Don't make a scene."

"Look at her. What will people think?"

"Nothing. Unless you make a federal case out of it."

He was right, of course. Chances are, no one else in all of Hurricane Beach would think twice about her mother sharing a cup of coffee with a visitor to town. Hurricane Beach was that kind of town; Helene Hardaway was that kind of woman, a one-woman welcome committee.

"But I asked him to keep a low profile," Amy protested. "Just until Spring Break is over. So the whole town doesn't get in an uproar."

"Having a cup of coffee with your mother isn't exactly taking out a billboard, Amy."

"You're too reasonable," she said. "That's your problem. You know that, don't you?"

She realized, as she snapped out the words, that her comment was directed at a lot more than the present situation. Look how reasonable, how rational, he'd been about this business of their relationship. He'd said they should be friends and he'd had absolutely no trouble whatsoever sticking to his guns.

Amy sighed. "Okay. Okay. I'll let it go. But you go back in there and keep an eye on him."

He smiled. "What do you think I was doing hanging out by the door in the middle of the day?"

The anger melted out of her, beginning with a small circle of warmth centered low in her body. "Really?"

"Really. What are friends for?"

*Friends.* The circle of warmth chilled to lukewarm. Amy wanted to kick him in the shins, but she didn't suppose the bare toes sticking out of her sandals would do much harm.

HELENE FELT HERSELF blush when Palmer Boyce said he shouldn't have been the least surprised when his landlady at the bed and breakfast told him Helene had once been on the stage.

"Your voice gives you away," he said. "And your carriage. I can't believe I didn't guess."

"Oh, my, but that was so long ago," she said, knowing she was fluttering her fingers in that silly way she did when she felt self-conscious. "And it was all very small-time, of course. USO and touring companies." She hesitated. "Except for Merrick, of course. He had quite the career, you know."

Darn Merrick, anyway. He'd been the one who'd so kindly pointed out that Palmer Boyce's interest in her was purely mercenary. Of course, Merrick was right.

And there he was spoiling things for her, just as he had all those years ago.

Fine for him. He'd had his moment of glory. Three seasons on that silly doctor show on TV, back in the days when TV was something. Live drama. Helene would have killed for a chance at live drama in the early days of television.

Darn Merrick, anyway.

Erasing the furrow she felt between her eyebrows, she turned her attention back to Palmer Boyce.

"But here you are buried in Hurricane Beach," he was saying. "How did this happen?"

She smiled sweetly, knowing she could still do this much acting, at least. "We decided it was time to raise a family, you see. And the theater is no place for bringing up children. Believe me, I know.''

''Really?''

He propped his chin on his fist and looked at her as if enthralled. Helene wondered how much acting Palmer Boyce might have done during his life. She remembered, for the first time, what Merrick had said all those years ago when he left the stage and started in real estate. Anyone who can act can sell, he'd said.

''Well, I do remember the final years of vaudeville,'' she said.

''Fascinating. Tell me about it, will you?''

Helene loved telling the old stories and she lost herself in them for a few minutes. Sleeping in trains while her parents ran lines and doing her lessons backstage and learning every bawdy comedy routine in the show by the age of nine. She'd been a hit at cast parties, delivering all the risqué lines she didn't understand. But she had loved the laughter and the applause. The theater was in her blood.

''Yet you haven't been on stage in years, I hear. Helene, that is a crime.''

''There are so few good roles for women of my age,'' she said. The admission reminded her how foolish she was being, flirting with a man fifteen years her junior. A man who wanted something from her, at that.

''Nonsense. You would steal the show.''

As she drove home forty-five minutes later, Helene found that the thrill of being flattered and pursued vanished quickly. The fact remained that the only man for Helene was Merrick.

She had done so much damage with her silly scheme. They were so distant now she couldn't even confide in him about Amy. And without Merrick to turn to, there was no one to tell.

"Oh, dear," she murmured, turning up the volume on the classical-music tape in hopes of drowning out her thoughts.

She and Merrick had reached a truce, it was true. But the truce felt shaky. Things at home were still tense. She especially hadn't liked the way he'd encouraged her to encourage Palmer Boyce.

"Wagging tongues will advance your little plot, don't you agree?" Merrick had said. "After all, 'the play's the thing,' if I recall."

The thing that troubled her the most was how much Merrick suddenly seemed to be enjoying their little charade. He didn't seem angry about it anymore and she hadn't even noticed when his attitude had changed. But one night, after Amy left, he'd even said he'd forgotten how invigorating performing could be. Helene, on the other hand, had never realized how wearing it was to be at cross-purposes with the man who owned your heart. Even if it was all an act.

Especially if you sometimes wondered if it was all an act.

She was a mile from the house when she saw a

shiny Mercedes passing, with Audrey Babcock at the wheel. Helene waved at the summer resident whose husband had passed away last summer, but Audrey didn't seem to see her.

Helene wondered what had brought Audrey back to Hurricane Beach, when she'd said last year she might never return without her Murray. She also wondered what the silver-blond widow was doing this far out of town. The only thing for miles in this direction was Sea Haven.

Could Audrey have been visiting Merrick?

Because she'd never had reason to experience it before, it took several hours and a conversation with Bea Connell before Helene recognized her feelings for what they were.

Jealousy.

AMY WAS LEAVING the YMCA after her weekly class when her mother's sports car pulled up to the curb and stopped. The passenger door was flung open in front of Amy and she leaned over to peer inside.

Helene stared straight ahead, the strangest expression on her face.

"Get in," she said. "I'll take you home."

Amy shifted her canvas bag of art supplies and tried to imagine where in her mother's small car she could stash it for the five-minute drive to her beach house. But there was a sharpness to Helene's tone that left no room for argument. Feeling suddenly uneasy, Amy climbed into the car and balanced her unwieldy bag on her lap.

The sports car left the curb with a roar, slamming Amy against the back of the seat: Her mouth felt dry.

"I just want you to listen," Helene said once they were on the beach highway. "I don't want to hear denials or excuses. For once, just listen and do as I say."

"Mom...?"

"I don't know how far this thing with Jon Costas has gone, but I want you to stop it. Now."

Fear and remorse welled up in Amy, choking her, making her hot and cold all at once.

"That man was your sister's husband," Helene said. "Lisa will be here in a matter of days. I won't have this family torn apart anymore."

Barely slowing, Helene spun into Amy's driveway, tires grinding on the crushed shells. She lurched to a stop, but still didn't turn to look at her daughter.

Amy found her voice, a strangled, broken sound. "But, Mom, it's not—"

"No, it's not. Not anymore. Are we clear on that point?"

"Mom, please—"

"Are we clear?"

Amy had never heard her mother sound this way, so cold, so implacable. "Yes, Mom. We're clear."

Helene drew a long breath and turned to Amy

with a smile. "Thank God. I knew I could count on you."

"Mom, I—"

Helene patted her hand. "No need to explain, dear. It's over. It never happened. Now, I'd better run along."


A HOLIDAY ATMOSPHERE arrived in Hurricane Beach the week before Spring Break. The streets were crowded with visitors and summer residents, all overburdened with shopping bags stuffed full of pottery and shell art and beachwear. A brightly painted banner went up across Gulfview welcoming everyone to Spring Break. Java Joe's unfurled a canopy and dragged its little tables onto the broad sidewalk. The florist rolled out a cart of fresh-cut tulips in exotic colors. Hurricane Beach was filled with a sense of excitement.

Only Amy Hardaway was finding it hard to get into the spirit of Spring Break.

Amy had spent the last week in purgatory. Helene refused to acknowledge their conversation about Jon Costas. It was, as Helene had said that day, as if it had never happened. But Amy wasn't that good an actress. She felt guilt. Oceans of guilt.

Driving with her parents to the Tallahassee airport to meet Megan's flight, her spirits temporarily lifted. The sun glowed softly, not yet the blistering, stifling instrument of heat it would be in another month or two. Helene and Merrick were quiet, the silence in the car filled with classical music, creating the illusion of serenity. Although Amy knew it was only an illusion—she'd never known her parents to go so long without a word between them, not in her entire life—she didn't fret over it, because she knew her sisters would be here soon. Between them, they would find the answers.

And with her sisters here, she would even be able to get her thoughts off Jon Costas. Wouldn't she?

On the drive back from the airport, however, the mood in the car shifted, beginning when Helene switched off the tape of classical music.

"Why did you do that?" Merrick asked, a little too sternly, Amy thought.

"So we can talk. For a change." The sharpness in Helene's reply was impossible to miss.

Amy glanced at Megan for her sister's reaction. Megan sat stiffly in her corner of the back seat, shoulders squared, ankles tightly crossed, hands clutched in her lap. At thirty-six, Megan's ash-blond hair still hung straight and smooth to her shoulders, untouched by a hint of gray. She might look younger than her years, but it was clear from the simply cut suit and classic gold earrings she wore that Megan strove for a mature image.

Megan looked out the window, but Amy saw her incline her head slightly in the direction of the front seat.

"We'll have plenty of time to talk when we reach

the house,'' Merrick said. "The music helps me concentrate on the highway.''

Helene pursed her lips. "Fine.'' She turned on the tape player, then glanced back at her daughters with a thin smile. "You girls go ahead and catch up. Megan can fill me in later.''

Amy nodded and tried to smile. Megan pursed her lips, a replica of their mother's expression, then returned to looking out the window.

THERE WAS very little catching up that night at dinner, either.

"Tell us how your job is going, dear,'' Helene asked as Annie served the she-crab soup.

"Oh, very well,'' Megan said, picking up her soup spoon before she seemed to realize that more news was expected of her. "Working with seniors is tremendously rewarding. And we're up for a grant to continue that music therapy program I instituted last year.''

"A grant?'' Helene's voice grew bright and she looked around the table. "Well, darling, that's wonderful. Isn't that wonderful, Merrick? That program she started may receive a grant.''

"I haven't lost my hearing yet, Helene.'' He turned to Megan with a warm, approving smile. "And yes, it is wonderful. When will you know?''

"Soon. A few weeks, I suppose.'' Megan sounded less excited about the possibility than either of her parents.

"That's lovely, dear," Helene said. "I'm so glad you haven't squandered your talents. As some of us have."

Merrick looked up, frowning darkly. "We're not going to get into that tonight, are we?"

"I'm not getting into anything," Helene said, pushing her soup to one side.

Amy felt the subtle escalation of tension and looked toward Megan, who said, "I hear Jon Costas is home."

Helene took her napkin out of her lap and folded it on the table in front of her. "All I meant to point out was that some of us had the opportunity to pursue our dreams and others of us did not."

Amy looked from one parent to another, then back at Megan. "Who told you that?"

"Why, Mother, I think."

And what else had Helene said? Amy wondered. "Mom…"

"I didn't say anything," Helene said.

"You wanted a family, too," Merrick said, taking a long swallow from his glass of wine. "Don't pretend this was my decision alone."

"Say anything about what?" Megan asked.

Everyone was looking at Helene now. She twisted her gold-knot earring and looked as if she desperately wanted to make this all go away. Instead, she pushed back from the table and stood. "I'm not feeling very well. If you don't mind, I think I'll excuse myself."

"Helene!" Merrick called after her the way he'd called after one of the girls as children, when they left the table without being excused. Then he looked at his daughters, folded his napkin and pushed back from the table, as well. "Your mother is...not herself. Please excuse me."

The two sisters stared across the table at each other, forlorn bookends who hadn't quite been able to prop things up.

"This is awful," Megan whispered. "He's being so irritable."

"Did you hear all those little digs she keeps making? She never did that before." Amy thought of the expression on her mother's face when she looked into Palmer Boyce's eyes and wondered what, exactly, was going on there. She thought of telling her sister, but hesitated. Why burden Megan?

Besides, one can of worms opened could lead to another.

"What's wrong with them?" Megan said. "They're acting like children."

"I know. Maybe it's this Silver Sands offer. If we get that resolved..."

Megan shook her head. "That's really none of our business, is it? Although I have to admit, I wouldn't be sorry to see the property gone."

Amy knew why her sister felt that way, and sympathized. But her own heart ached at the thought. She remembered every inch of this beach, these dunes, and the games they had played on them as children. How could either of her sisters bear to see the place gone? "Lisa seems to think we can get it resolved."

"Oh, dear. I really don't want to get in the middle of any unpleasantness."

"Our parents are at each other's throats. It's not likely to be pleasant."

"Maybe I ought to go home."

"No. Please. You have to stay. We have to do what we can."

Amy saw Megan's reluctance in the way her sister studied the ice in her glass while rolling the stem between her fingers. "Okay. I just want to go on record as saying I don't want a lot of turmoil."

Amy refrained from pointing out that things had been nothing but turmoil in Hurricane Beach for months. And they showed no sign of getting better on their own. "I understand."

They finished their soup in silence. It was cold, but neither said a word, until Megan said, "Lisa's going to have a conniption about Jon Costas."

Amy's heart skipped a beat. "Why do you say that?"

Megan shrugged. "I just always thought she never got over him. Why else would she bury herself up there in New England, for heaven's sake?"

"You think she's still in love with him?"

"Well, I think she's carrying a torch for somebody. Who else could it be?"

# CHAPTER THIRTEEN

WALKING HOME along the deserted beach that night, Amy pondered her sister's words. *Who else could it be?* The only face that came to mind was the lean, sun-bronzed face of Jon Costas.

She wasn't surprised to see him sitting in the gazebo. She slowed and studied him. He leaned against the railing, staring at the surf. His shoulders were just square enough, his waist just trim enough to make him perfect, in her eyes. His silver hair always did something to her, as did his coffee-brown eyes and his wide, infectious smile.

But it wasn't his looks that made him so hard to put out of her mind.

It was the way he listened to her, and asked her questions. It was his devotion to his niece, even when she was difficult, and his gentle way with his family, especially because she knew how much they irritated him. It didn't matter. Bottom line, they were family and he loved them and he wouldn't hurt them for the world.

Yes, the very act of coming home, giving up his old life simply because his family needed him, that was one of the things that made Jon Costas the kind of man she couldn't look at once and keep moving.

Those were the things she loved about Jon Costas.

She smiled and started toward him, realizing the full implication of her thoughts only when he turned and saw her. *The things she loved?* She froze in her tracks, just as his irresistible smile kicked in.

"Amy."

The way he said her name, so soft and welcoming, even that touched something deep inside her.

But love?

It couldn't be. Never.

Once again, Megan's words came back to her. *Who else could it be?*

"I didn't mean to interrupt," she said, already plotting her retreat. What if Helene found out?

He held out a hand to her. "Select company is welcome."

"I'd better get home." Of course, there was no one to tell Helene. And she *was* an adult. And Jon was only a *friend.* There was nothing wrong with loving your friends.

"Take a few minutes," he said. "There's supposed to be a comet tonight."

"It's late." And that was lame.

"Fifteen minutes."

She was ready to give in.

"I'll walk you home."

That did it. "No, I don't think so."

"How'd it go with Megan tonight?"

The pull of someone to listen made it easy to ignore the warnings in her head. She took a few steps in his direction. "Not so good."

"Sorry."

"She doesn't want any turmoil." Amy smiled wryly as she stepped into the gazebo and sat on the railing, facing him. *Who else could it be?* The thought haunted her. "Mom and Dad were sniping at each other all night. All the way back from the airport."

"I don't think I ever saw them argue in all the years I was...in all the years I knew them," he said. "Think it would help to run Palmer Boyce out of town on a rail?"

"I think that's what they call treating a symptom."

He looked at her, a searching look that left her heart racing.

"Sometimes treating a symptom is exactly what we need," he said.

She didn't really want to know what he meant by that. She didn't really want to examine these feelings she was having—the physical sensations, the emotional longings. She needed to weed them out, be rid of them once and for all. She tried to think of a way to do that.

"Want to come with me to pick up Lisa at the airport?"

"Is that a good idea?"

She thought of having him in the car with her all

the way to Tallahassee. Being near him. Hearing his voice. Inhaling the spicy, bake-shop scent of him. She thought of what her mother would say. A good idea? She shook her head. "I have no idea."

It must have been the right answer, because Jon laughed and agreed to come. But only if she let him walk her home. She agreed, telling herself she had to guard against any overtures he might make. With Lisa's arrival just days away, she couldn't run the risk of any touches, any kisses.

He made no overtures for her to guard against. She walked into the house alone and felt inexplicably disappointed.

MERRICK STOOD on the small balcony off their bedroom and gazed into the night sky, then at his watch. When the time was right, he walked back inside and over to the bed, where Helene was pretending to sleep.

"Come see the comet," he said softly, sitting beside her on the bed. "It's just about time."

He saw her eyes tighten as she strove to maintain the illusion of sleep. He smiled.

"Come, my dear, you're not that good an actress," he said, hoping she wouldn't miss the teasing he intended.

"No," she said, her tone cold. "I suppose not. I never really had the opportunity, did I?"

Merrick felt stung. He also felt as if the woman who had been his most constant, his most intimate companion for almost fifty years had become a stranger. "Helene, where is this coming from? This bitterness?"

Her answer broke his heart, for it made him wonder how he could have failed her so and never realized it.

"I'm not sure, Merrick. Maybe it's always been there."

He got up and went back out, fighting tears. Fighting fears. The comet didn't look as brilliant, or as miraculous, as he had expected moments before. The foundation of his life was crumbling and he had no idea how to stop it from happening.

"Help," he whispered into the darkness. "Please help."

MEGAN WALKED along Gulfview, feeling vulnerable, fragile in a way she hadn't experienced in a long time. Being at the family house had made her uneasy. Seeing her parents feud made her feel unsafe, and Megan craved safety the way others craved liquor or chocolate or a good book on a rainy night.

But no matter how safe she managed to make her life seem, nothing could bring her son back.

And that, she thought, was why she hated coming back to Hurricane Beach. Whenever she was here, the pain felt as new and as devastating as it had been all those years ago.

She continued her walk along Gulfview, looking for familiar faces, concentrating on the changes in the shops since her visit last summer. Java Joe's had added the striped canopy. The florist's had spruced up its pushcart. A sandwich board sat outside the café listing the day's specials, something she'd never seen in Hurricane Beach before.

She had reached the end of the business district and planned to turn around and go back to Rêve Rags, when she saw the Greyhound bus. It had stopped, as usual, at the service station, belching fumes and making more noise with its rumbling engine than Hurricane Beach was accustomed to. Megan thought about crossing to the other side of the street to get away from the fumes.

Then he stepped off the bus.

He carried a worn blue duffel bag. He was dressed like a teenager—torn jeans, loud-colored T-shirt sporting an off-color message, unkempt hair pulled back in a ponytail—but he wasn't a teenager. Closer to thirty, she would have guessed. He looked up and down the street, a purposeful, searching look that made Megan shiver.

He was obviously a stranger in town. Just as the person who'd walked away with her son must have been.

He started in the direction Megan was headed. She froze, letting him get ahead of her, unwilling to get too close.

*You're being foolish,* she told herself. *Overreacting. The way you used to. Just because you're here, in Hurricane Beach. There must be lots of new faces here by now. You wouldn't even notice him if you were back home. You see people like him every day.*

Still, both hands clutched the strap of the purse she wore slung over her shoulder. Her nails cut into her palms and no amount of positive self-talk could convince her to ease her grip.

She hoped he would reach his destination soon, get off the street, out of her line of vision.

*Let it go,* she told herself. *Don't slip back into paranoia again. Don't do it.*

The man finally paused in front of one of the shops, pressed his face to the window and peered in. Megan's step faltered. She didn't want to catch up with him.

Then he waved to someone inside, winked and continued walking. He picked up his pace and turned off Gulfview moments later. As soon as he was gone, Megan's breathing eased.

It was only when she reached Rêve Rags, where she'd promised to visit Grace, that she realized her sister's shop was where the man had paused to wave and wink.

So he wasn't a complete stranger, she told herself. Obviously he knew one of Amy's customers. So there was no reason in the world for Megan to be concerned.

AMY HAD second thoughts about taking Jon to the airport with her. Second thoughts about the wisdom of spending that much time alone with him. Second thoughts about Helene's reaction, especially after she'd seen the look Helene and Megan had exchanged when Amy stopped by Sea Haven for breakfast.

"Why on earth would you do that?" Megan had said, and it was clear from her disapproving look that Helene had explained things to her older daughter sometime after Amy left the night before.

Amy, of course, had worked out her explanation on the way over that morning. "Because I think Mom is right. There may still be feelings between the two of them. And I doubt if Lisa would seek Jon out on her own."

"Well, you're probably right about that," Megan had said.

But Helene had looked pleased.

Amy felt fidgety all the way to the airport. The conversation between her and Jon was start-and-stop. Amy kept punching buttons on the car radio, looking for the music that would provide the perfect distraction. She missed her turnoff. She chewed both thumbnails to the quick.

For the truth was, Amy needed this moment. Needed to see what would happen between Lisa and Jon in that instant when they first laid eyes on each other. She had to see firsthand what each of them would reveal in that unguarded moment.

On the way up and while waiting for the plane to land, Jon had been pleasant to the point of seeming unconcerned. He'd talked about the bakery and Kieran and the way his *theo* Nikos had quietly canvassed the Greek community in North Florida to help out an elderly Greek woman from Jacksonville who'd been taken for her life savings by a flimflam artist.

But Amy could tell from the way he kept reaching up to straighten a necktie he wasn't wearing that Jon's nerves were stretched taut as they waited for the passengers to disembark.

"There she is!" Amy pointed toward the slim woman striding confidently through the crowd, but her eyes were on Jon.

He looked the way he always looked when she most wanted to know what he was thinking. Inscrutable. Expressionless. He didn't smile. He didn't frown. He didn't clutch his chest and look faint.

It occurred to Amy that Jon shut down this way anytime he was confronted by a situation in which he felt unsure of himself. Better not to react at all, perhaps, than to react the wrong way.

Giving up trying to read his reaction, she waved broadly and called to her sister, noisy, attention-getting actions that she realized instantly irritated her sedate younger sister. Lisa wore tailored linen slacks and a contrasting blazer over a silk blouse in a muted color that played up her dark brown eyes. Amy grinned to smooth things over and hide her nervousness. She stopped short of giving Lisa a big hug.

"And look what I brought. A surprise." She gestured toward Jon.

For once, Lisa's cool failed her. Dismay filled her eyes, followed instantly by anger. Her tone, however, was unemotional. "What are you doing here?"

Was anger masking Lisa's real feelings? Amy asked herself. There didn't seem to be any sign of excitement. Not even an instant of delight at the sight of her ex-husband that she had to rush to hide. No longing or intimacy or pain. That was good, wasn't it? Amy realized her own emotions were so high she couldn't be sure what was going on with her sister. "I invited him."

Lisa took a moment, then she said, with the barest hint of irony, "What a nice surprise. My ex-husband as a welcome committee."

Now Jon smiled and Amy cast another glance at her sister, wondering how any woman could resist that smile.

"Amy thought you'd feel better knowing I've gotten old and gray," Jon said.

Lisa showed no sign of melting over the smile. "Oh, it does my heart good. I trust I caused a few of those."

He leaned over, pointing to the top of his head. "This whole bunch here, I think. And maybe a few over this ear."

He and Amy laughed. But Amy's mouth was dry and something in the region of her heart was beginning to hurt, sharp little jabs of discomfort that made her want to lie down in her hammock and shut out everything but the sound of the waves and the gulls and an occasional snore from Sam.

Jon offered to carry Lisa's single bag, but she told him she could manage and they headed for the car, Lisa in the middle. Amy wanted to be careful that way. Because now that she'd seen them together and saw no major attraction, no sign of eternal regret, she was convinced that the reactions would begin once the shock wore off.

Then, she thought, they would realize what they'd been denying all these years.

And she didn't want to be in the middle when that realization struck.

LISA SAT in the front seat. With the driver. Her ex-husband. An arrangement her meddling sister had insisted upon.

Amy was nothing if not transparent.

And one of the things Lisa could see very clearly was that Amy attached great significance to this little reunion between Lisa and Jon. Lisa almost smiled. How could Amy know that Jon Costas was not the man Lisa thought of whenever she thought of her old hometown?

Besides, she had a new man in her life. A good, solid man. The last thing she was interested in was the one who, thankfully, had got away.

"Megan's already here," Amy said. Small talk.

Lisa reciprocated. "How is she?"

"Fine. Well, she's worried about Mom and Dad. I am, too."

Lisa glanced at Jon, then into the back seat at her sister. "Why don't we talk about this later."

"Sure. I told her we would. That the three of us could work this out."

"Later, Amy."

Jon smiled. Lisa had hated that smile the last year they were married, because he'd seemed to flash it for everyone but her. Now, she discovered, it didn't affect her at all. What a relief. Not that she'd ever really thought otherwise. Still, it was nice to have it confirmed.

"It's not exactly a family secret," Jon said.

"Nevertheless…"

"He's right," Amy said. "About the fighting, at least."

"The Silver Sands deal," Jon said. "I don't think anybody's heard about that yet."

"How do *you* know about this?" Lisa asked him, finding the easy familiarity between Jon and her sister a little irritating.

"I have my ways."

"That's a good question," Amy said. "You never did say who told you."

Jon hesitated. "I just…checked around."

The car grew uncomfortably warm, Lisa thought. She adjusted the air-conditioning vent. "This is really none of your business, Jon."

"Hurricane Beach is my town, too." His good

humor seemed unfazed by her disapproval. That had always irritated her, too.

"Amy, can't we table this whole discussion?"

"I'm not a security leak," Jon said amiably.

"He's known for weeks and hasn't told a soul," Amy said.

"That's not really the issue."

Jon said, "What is the issue?"

"This is family business," Lisa said. "And you are not family."

"Ah." He nodded, as if he understood and accepted. He'd always been like that. Unflappable. Nothing disturbed him. Nothing threw him for a loop. Cool, calm and collected, ever reminding Lisa that her own cool was nothing but surface. She'd always been afraid that he could see beneath that surface, to the insecurities and inadequacies.

The silence in the car, a silence that felt tense and charged with unresolved emotions, lasted only seconds. Then Amy, irrepressible Amy, said, "Tell Jon about your work, Lisa. He's been dying to hear about it. Haven't you, Jon?"

Jon smiled again. "Dying."

Lisa could only wish.

## CHAPTER FOURTEEN

SAME OLD LISA, Jon thought as he watched the two sisters drive away. Beautiful but distant. Bright but unbending. With the right person, he supposed, she could open up, lighten up.

The right person wasn't him. Never had been.

The difference between Amy and Lisa was night and day. And a part of him couldn't help mourning that, as much as he'd yearned to be close to Lisa, something about him had always had the opposite effect on her. Maybe they'd been too much alike— both determined their way was the right way. Both had been too guarded with their emotions—and too young to know how to fix things.

But Amy, now Amy was a different batch of phyllo, as Aurelia would say.

Amy's emotions flowed freely, and that helped Jon loosen up, too. Amy was always so darned enthusiastic about everything she pursued, and that made him want to give in and let her have things her way. And that was good for him, too.

Except when it made him do stupid things, like agreeing with her crazy notion that they should be friends.

Well, now he knew better.

His thoughts turned to his meeting the first of the week with Dexter Garland. If things panned out the way he hoped, he'd be out of Hurricane Beach before too long. He'd spoken with Garland a few days earlier and learned that he was establishing international headquarters in South Florida. And he'd been so impressed with Jon's work at the brokerage firm, he wanted to talk with Jon about coming in as vice president of finance.

The opportunity was too good to be true. Just thinking about it should excite him. Freedom from family, plenty of money, all the allure of South Florida. It was everything he'd fantasized about when he lived in Manhattan.

He'd meant to tell Amy the night before, but she'd been so upset about her parents. He would tell her soon. Before he left.

Because another thought kept intruding on his plans. Given how he felt about Amy, how could he go off and leave her? He couldn't. It was that simple. And the solution that came to mind was equally simple.

The idea panicked him. Had he lost his mind?

How could he even *think* about marrying his ex-sister-in-law?

KIERAN FELT a little breathless rushing down the beach in the dark to meet Hardball. She'd never been this far down the beach so late at night, and things seemed eerie. The roar of the waves was louder, more menacing. And she could hear things rustling in the grass on the nearby dunes. She worried about jellyfish that might have washed up on the beach, and nameless things that held even bigger terrors.

But she knew Hardball would be waiting, right where she'd told him.

When the old pier with its weathered, ramshackle building came into view, she began to run faster. By the time she reached the edge of the water, she was calling his name. She waded into the cold, dark water and groped for the ladder onto the pier.

Why hadn't she thought to bring a flashlight?

And why hadn't Hardball answered when she called a moment ago?

Telling herself this was no time to act like a baby, Kieran started reluctantly up the ladder. She tested each step carefully, remembering that some were loose, a few had rotted through. The dank smell of rotting wood filled her nostrils, seemed to clog her lungs.

"Hardball?" she called, more softly this time, some of her earlier exuberance waning.

The six rungs of the ladder took forever. By the time she reached the door to the little shed, her heart was thumping and a sob threatened to jar loose from her chest.

Where was Hardball?

He sat lounging against a wall, legs crossed,

smoking a cigarette. Kieran's heart took a leap, her apprehension instantly vanished.

"Hardball!"

"Hi, Beach Bunny."

He sounded exactly the way she'd expected him to—laid-back and cool. She wanted to run and throw her arms around him. But she knew better than to act like some hyper child.

"I can't believe you're here." She dropped to her knees beside him.

"Would I let you down, Bunny?"

"Of course not."

He turned heavy-lidded eyes on her and studied her up and down. She held her breath.

"You're a cute little bunny, honey. What's your real name?"

She told him, watched his lazy grin. She'd been unable to make out his features when he'd waved at her through the front window at Rêve Rags. Up close, he didn't look exactly the way she'd expected him to. He was older, for one thing. His long hair was pulled back into a ponytail, but even in the moonlight she could tell it was thinning on top. His rumpled clothes hung on a bony frame. His cheeks sucked in when he drew off his cigarette, the dark bristle disappearing into darker hollows beneath his sharp cheekbones.

He held the cigarette out to her. She almost took it because she didn't want him to think her uncool. Then she remembered the cigarette she'd stolen from her dad one night. It had made her so sick she'd thrown up. Definitely uncool. She shook her head.

"So, how old is Kieran Costas?"

She'd already pondered the pros and cons of telling him the truth. Fifteen sounded so lame. "Seventeen."

His gaze once again strayed over her. "Don't sweat it. You'll grow." He ruffled the hair she had cropped off when she decided that dreadlocks didn't fit the scenery at Rêve Rags. "Besides, you're one smart little bunny rab. Tell me about the bank account."

She told him how much money she'd managed to hoard.

"That is outstanding," he said, flipping the butt of his cigarette off the end of his thumb, sending it flying through the darkness. Amy hoped the wood in the old shed was too damp to burn. "Do you have any idea how far a smart girl like you can go?"

"I couldn't have done it without you, Hardball. Say, I don't even know your real name."

He grinned and put his hands up to pillow his head against the wall. "What do you say we take a little trip?"

"A trip?"

"On that much money, we could make it to L.A."

"California?"

"Two people like us, we could make a mark in L.A."

The idea at once excited and frightened Kieran. No more school. No more grandparents fighting over her. She could show them all. She could simply walk away one day, and they would know, once and for all, that they didn't own her. She wondered if they would all act as crazy as everyone had acted when her old man disappeared.

Think of the way people would talk.

She thought of Uncle Jon, who at least wouldn't have that weighed-down look he seemed to get in his eyes every time he looked at her. He could take that new job she'd overheard him discussing on the phone without feeling guilty. She thought of Grandma, who babied her to death. She thought of Grace, who sometimes looked at her in a way that made her think she must look a lot like her worthless excuse for a father.

She thought of Amy.

That one bothered her. She put that thought away for now.

Hardball was spinning a tale of L.A. Parties and celebrities and glamour. "A girl with your looks, you could stand them on their ear. I'm a good manager, you know."

"A manager?" Kieran breathed the word reverently. "Is that what you are, a manager?"

"I'm not talking starring vehicles. Not at first. A few walk-ons. Maybe a line or two. But it wouldn't take long. I've got a friend, could cook up a line on you—"

"A line?"

"Yeah. A life history. For image. Wouldn't take much, Brad Pitt would be on the phone every day, trying to get you for his next flick."

"Really?" The images danced in her head, intoxicating and alluring.

He put a finger under her chin and turned her face to study her profile. "Never doubt, honey-bunny. Never doubt the man."

"You'd do that for me?"

"I've done it for women with less to offer than you."

*Women.* He'd practically called her a woman. A thrill skittered through Kieran.

"Or, we could work a few gigs in L.A., save up and go to Australia. You ever been to the Outback?"

Kieran shook her head, enthralled.

"Paradise. They haven't screwed it up the way they've screwed things up here. There's miles and miles of virgin land, animals roaming free under an endless sky. You up to being a frontier bunny?"

"It sounds wonderful."

"Yeah. I thought so."

He spun tales for hours about the virtues of the fast life in L.A. versus the unfettered freedom of the Outback. Each scenario he created sounded better than the one before. And by the time Kieran crept back down the ladder, her head was spinning with possibilities. Imagine, spending her life with a man who knew how to dream, a man who wasn't bound by all the rigid limits found in a place like Hurricane Beach.

She was halfway home before she realized he never had said what his real name was.

Never mind. There was plenty of time for that.

GIRLS' NIGHT OUT. A sleep-over. Amy realized pretty quickly that her big plans for bringing her two sisters together under her roof were going to be a bust.

"We should have stayed with Mom and Dad," Megan fretted, drying and putting away the glasses that Amy usually let dry overnight in the dish drainer.

"Mom and Dad will be fine," Amy said.

"That's why we came back, isn't it?" Megan said. "For them? Then shouldn't we be there?"

"We'd have more room," Lisa said as she rearranged the silverware in Amy's messy drawer into the neat compartments Amy always intended to use but never quite got around to. "Goodness knows, there's no reason for us to camp out all over your place when there are plenty of bedrooms at Sea Haven."

"I just thought it would be fun," Amy said. "That's all. You know. The way it used to be."

Megan smiled at her, the kind of smile a nurse might give a particularly deluded patient. Lisa didn't even look up from her task, merely shook her head.

"We were kids then," Lisa said. "We're grown-up. It's different."

"But it doesn't have to be. Does it?"

Lisa shut the drawer. Megan put the last glass on the shelf and closed the cabinet.

"More wine, anybody?" Lisa said, picking up the bottle from the table and splashing a bit into her wineglass.

Megan begged off. Amy took another swallow or two, in the spirit of companionship. As her two sisters wandered through the living room and onto the deck, she doubted it was worth the effort.

She followed them. The moon was new, a bare sliver in the dark sky. Perfect for tomorrow night's fireworks.

She wondered what Jon was doing tonight. A sense of longing sprang up in her.

"We should have a strategy," she said, determined to shake all thoughts of Jon. "For talking to Mom and Dad about the Silver Sands offer. Make a united stand, don't you think?"

As she glanced from one to the other, a united stand seemed a very remote possibility. Lisa looked so confident, so mature. And Meagan looked soft, almost girlish, with her long hair pulled back in a ponytail. Lisa seemed more like their father every day, Megan more like Helene.

"We should tell them to sell," Lisa said decisively. "Get this over and done with and there's nothing more to squabble over."

"Is that all Sea Haven is to you?" Amy said softly. "Something to squabble over?"

"I agree with Lisa," Megan said, pulling her feet tightly against her in the lounge chair she'd chosen. Even in a lounge chair, she looked protective of herself. "I'd be glad to see the property gone."

Lisa chose a seat on the bench built into the railing. "Good. That's settled."

"Wait," Amy said. "I didn't agree."

Lisa shrugged. "Majority rules. Isn't that the way it works?"

"Amy, we're not trying to shove anything down your throat," Megan said. "But look at all the trouble this is causing. Selling will keep the peace. Don't you think?"

"We're talking about selling the place where we grew up. Doesn't that make anybody but me sad?"

Apparently not. Neither of her sisters bothered to reply.

"But everything will change," she went on. Surely she could make them see things her way.

"Everything's already changed," Lisa told her.

That was painfully obvious. Amy remembered the way the three of them had been twenty years ago, when they'd huddled together in one bedroom late into the night, despite the fact they'd each had a separate room. They would go off to bed and an hour later one of them would sneak up and wander into another bedroom. Soon, the third sister would join them as if by prior agreement and they would sit up whispering about the best movie they'd seen lately or a new plan for stunting their growth so they didn't end up taller than all the boys in the class. Often, Helene would find them the next morning, draped all over the floor or the bed or the window seat in one bedroom, still snoozing in the spot where sleep had overtaken them.

And now, here they were hiding behind these masks they'd developed over the years to keep one another at bay. Megan, working so hard to make sure no one's feathers were ruffled, that nothing be allowed to disturb the calm life she wanted. Lisa, as ever the controlled perfectionist.

And to them, Amy supposed, she still looked like the little girl who never grew up. The Peter Pan of the Hardaway girls, whining because things have changed.

*Can they see beneath my mask any better than I can see beneath theirs?* she wondered. Could they tell that underneath the breezy clothes and the hair she refused to cut and the earrings made of wrecked car metal that she was lonely? She desperately wanted to revive the closeness they so long ago rejected.

She thought of telling them exactly that. She sat in the silence for a few moments, wondering whether to risk further rejection, and said, "Are either of you lonely sometimes?"

"I'm around people all the time," Megan said softly. "There isn't time for that."

Why, then, did she sound unspeakably lonely when she said it?

Lisa swallowed the last of her wine and stood. "I'll take the sofa. Meggie, you can have the spare room."

Megan drifted off, too. Amy sat listening to the surf a while longer, wondering how they had all reached the point where it was so hard to share their real feelings.

She wondered whether any of them would ever have the courage to change.

## CHAPTER FIFTEEN

FIREWORKS STARTED early on the final morning of Spring Break.

The three sisters walked the four miles down the beach to Sea Haven to meet their parents for the drive into town for the day-long festivities. Before they even left Amy's house, they were bickering.

"This is all you have for breakfast?" Megan said, wrinkling her nose over the basket of fresh pastries.

"What's wrong with it?" Amy said, bringing out milk and sugar for their coffee.

Megan looked at the nutritional label on the milk and frowned. "You don't have skim?"

"Come on," Lisa said, grabbing a sweet roll. "Just eat and let's go."

"Jon made those, you know," Amy told her.

Lisa paused to examine the pastry.

"It's not poisoned," Amy said.

"You're sure?"

Megan poured the barest splash of milk into her coffee and said, "That's a matter of opinion. Do you have any idea what happens to your blood-sugar level when you start your day with...this...this...stuff?"

"Instant energy?" Amy said brightly.

"We don't really want to know, Meggie."

Megan was undaunted. She explained it while they ate and was still lecturing them halfway down the beach.

It was probably the most pleasant conversation they were to have the rest of the day.

When Merrick and Helene came out of the house, Lisa started on them before they even reached the car.

"Let's get this out of the way so it doesn't spoil the day," Lisa said.

Helene and Merrick stopped and glanced at each other. Amy shifted her canvas bag to the other shoulder and braced for the disagreement. Megan said, "Oh, Lisa—"

"We think you should sell," Lisa said.

"Sell what?" Helene said.

"Sea Haven, of course," Merrick said stiffly. "You didn't think for one minute they wouldn't find out, did you?"

"But—"

Amy leaned toward her mother. "Actually, we don't—"

Lisa plowed on, giving her sister a pointed look. "We discussed it last night and we wanted to present a united front and encourage you to sell."

"Actually, we didn't—"

"Do we have to talk about this now?" Megan said.

Merrick looked at his wife and said, "You see."

Helene shook her head. "I don't think they understand all the implications, Merrick. Now, if we could all sit down and—"

Amy glanced at her watch. "We need to get going. All the good spots on the beach will be gone."

Megan opened the car door and held it open for Lisa. "She's right. So is Mother. Let's table this discussion for another time. Couldn't we just have a nice time today?"

Lisa walked around the car to open her own door. "Don't forget, I'm leaving first thing in the morning."

"You're welcome to stay longer," Amy said, suddenly struck with a vision of touring the property with her sisters, to remind them what everyone would be losing by selling. "We could pack a picnic and—"

"I really have to be back at work," Lisa said, getting in the car and closing her door.

"Well, one day—"

"Let's not argue," Megan said, giving Amy a pleading look.

Amy sighed. She slid into the back seat next to Lisa and Megan got in beside her. She'd always ended up sitting in the middle, it seemed to her. As a child, she'd liked it that way. It had made her feel close to both her sisters.

It didn't work that way today.

They sat in the back seat for a moment before

anyone realized that their parents were still standing in front of the car. The low rumble of their father's voice reached them. And the tremulous look on their mother's face spoke silent volumes, as well.

"They're fighting," Megan said.

"I told you we should decide this and get it over with," Lisa said.

"Let me out," Amy said. "Maybe I can smooth things over."

Nobody moved.

"I said—"

"This is between them," Lisa said. "It's none of our business."

"Only if we're not a family anymore," Amy snapped.

"It won't help if we're all fighting, too," Megan said softly.

Lisa frowned at the wide-brimmed straw hat Amy wore. "Is that thing necessary? It's taking up half the back seat."

"If somebody lets me out, it won't take up any room."

Lisa chuckled and opened her door. "Okay, White Knight. Save the day."

When Amy emerged from the car, Helene was saying, "Then I'll just stay home."

She marched toward the house. Amy trotted behind her. "Mother, please. Lisa and Megan are here. All three of us are together. You know how long it's been since we were all together?"

"And you've certainly done your part to make sure harmony reigns, haven't you?"

Her mother's words stung like a slap to the face. Even Merrick looked stunned by Helene's response. "Helene, for God's sake, where's the good in turning on Amy?"

Helene paused and squeezed her eyes shut. "Oh, Amy, I'm sorry."

Amy shrugged and told herself those were not tears collecting in her eyes. She cleared her throat. "That's okay, Mom. Listen, we'll talk about Sea Haven tonight, after we get home. Who knows, if we have a nice day, maybe it'll all seem a lot simpler by then."

"Do you think?" Helene looked as if she desperately wanted to believe that.

"Stranger things have happened." Amy gave her mother her most convincing smile.

The two women linked arms and walked the few steps back to the car.

"No talk of selling Sea Haven," Helene announced. "The topic is banished until tonight. After the fireworks."

Megan looked relieved. Merrick looked doubtful. Lisa managed to look amused but unconcerned. As Amy climbed back into the car, Lisa murmured, "Let the fireworks begin."

No one was in a holiday mood.

They stabbed a couple of umbrellas into the sand

and staked off family territory, as others were doing up and down the beach. If the Hardaways weren't feeling festive, at least the town and its residents and visitors were doing their best to make things look cheerful. Brightly striped umbrellas dotted the beach. Lawn chairs of every color and description lined the pier. A small hot-air balloon hovered over the marina, brightening both the sky and the faces of children. Pushcarts were everywhere, offering hot dogs and snow cones and fresh pastries from the Costas Family Bakery. Gulfview Lane was open only to foot traffic, and as early as it was, people were already streaming along the street, checking out the booths of games and crafts.

"Isn't this wonderful?" Amy said. "Just like the old days."

Helene was the only one who returned her smile.

"I'm going for the morning paper," Merrick said.

"But Dad—" Surely he didn't plan to hide behind the newspaper today, Amy thought.

"In 'the old days,' I was fourteen," Lisa said, dropping into a chair under one of the umbrellas.

Amy refused to allow her smile to fade. "Come on, Lisa, let's sign up for the three-legged sand race. I'll bet Grace and I can beat you and Megan."

Megan glanced up and down the beach as if to keep an eye on everyone. "I do all the racing I need at Graceway."

"Okay," Amy said. "How about the sand-castle competition, then? The team that builds the best sand castle wins a kite from Up In the Air. What do you say?''

"Isn't that the Costas family?'' Megan said.

Amy looked in the direction Megan gestured, but not before she glanced at her younger sister. Lisa's unruffled expression never changed.

Sure enough, the entire Costas clan had descended on the stretch of unclaimed beach nearest the Hardaways. With six umbrellas, nineteen chairs of various types and a giant cooler, they could easily become their very own private celebration.

Except that the Costas family was seldom quiet enough to do anything privately.

Aurelia appeared to spot the Hardaways first. But not before Amy had pinpointed Jon. In the crowd of noisy, dark-haired people, his silver hair stood out, glinting in the sun and drawing her eye.

Like gnats after cocoa butter, she thought. The draw was irresistible.

He wore khaki shorts and a loose-fitting white cotton shirt, its sleeves rolled halfway up his forearms and its banded collar open. Would Lisa notice how wonderful he looked?

But when she glanced at her sister, Lisa was staring at her.

Grateful for her oversize hat and its floppy brim, Amy ducked her head to avoid the scrutiny.

"Good heavens,'' Megan said. "They've certainly multiplied, haven't they?''

"Watch out,'' Lisa said. "Isn't this Aurelia,

headed our way? Maybe we *should* go sign up for one of the races.''

''Hush,'' Amy said.

''Oh, my, can you believe it!'' Aurelia turned back toward her family and called out, ''Leda, come here. This you won't believe. All the Hardaway girls. All here at once. Come, they don't look a day over nineteen.''

Leda looked over and frowned, hands on her hips. Amy thought for a moment she wouldn't come. But Aurelia kept calling to her until Jon's mother gave up and walked over.

''Why, so it is,'' she said. ''All the Hardaway girls.''

She nodded politely at Megan. ''A nurse, I hear. Good for you, you do God's work.'' Then she let her gaze drift quickly over Lisa. ''And Lisa. So good to see you, Lisa.''

''And you,'' Lisa said.

Amy would have been hard-pressed to say who behaved with more cool civility.

''And my girl Amy,'' Leda said with a big smile. ''This girl, you won't believe what she does with my grandbaby. That girl, she's a hobo until Amy comes along. A bum, this is how she dresses. Listens to nobody. Until Amy.''

And she wrapped her arms around Amy and gave her the trademark Costas family hug. Over Leda's shoulder, Amy once again caught Lisa's sardonic gaze.

"That's my sis," Lisa said. "Always saving the day."

Leda and Aurelia pursed their lips and looked at each other. Amy searched Lisa's face for some hint of affection in the comment. Before she could decide if there was, three of the Costas grandchildren stormed through, calling out to one another and upturning Megan's totebag of sunscreen and burn spray and the extra visor she'd brought just in case.

Lisa looked irritated with the interruption; Megan looked away, but not before Amy caught the longing in her older sister's eyes as her gaze followed the disruptive children.

Close on their trail came Kieran, who paused and rolled her eyes at Amy. "And I'm supposed to be watching them today. Some fun."

Then she was off, too, looking adorable in the tie-dyed beach cover Grace had set aside for her.

"Ah, the next generation," Aurelia said fondly.

"Good morning, ladies."

Merrick, returning from his search for the paper, sounded his usual gracious self. He dropped the paper into the chair farthest from the one Helene had claimed, and tipped his canvas hat.

"Oh, Mr. Hardaway, my husband is wanting a word with you," Leda said, turning to call Demetri.

"Not now, Leda," Aurelia said.

"And why not now, I want to know? Is this not the only time the lot of us see one another?"

Aurelia looked uncomfortable, and glanced at Amy apologetically.

Demetri came across the short expanse of beach that separated the families, looking almost comical in his baggy shorts and tropical-print shirt.

"Ah, the Hardaway family. Mrs. Hardaway. Girls." He nodded politely, then turned his attention to Merrick. "Mr. Hardaway, my family talks and we want you to know—"

Nikos came up at that moment and put a hand on his brother's burly shoulder. "Now, Deme?"

"And why not now, I want to know?"

Aurelia rolled her eyes. "This is what I say to Leda. Not now." She looked at Amy for support. "Don't I say this myself?"

"What's on your mind, Mr. Costas?" Merrick said. "Now is as good a time as any."

"We are believing this big Silver Sands project is a good idea," Demetri said. "Lots of business for all, we think."

"Well, not all of us think this," Aurelia muttered.

"See, Mom," Lisa said. "The whole town probably agrees."

"No, they don't," Amy said. "Dad, you know better than that. You know how the merchants' association feels about this kind of development."

"Nikos, he's on the association, and he agrees," Demetri said.

From the corner of her eye, Amy noticed that Jon

had wandered over. Relief flooded her, as if his presence alone could keep this squabble from escalating.

"This really isn't about what the merchants' association thinks anyway," Helene observed.

"No, it isn't," Merrick said. "We appreciate your concern, Mr. Costas, but this is a family matter."

"A family matter?" Demetri's voice rose. "A family matter for all the families in Hurricane Beach, is how I see it."

Jon said, "Pop, why don't—"

"Family!" Aurelia pointed sharply at Deme. "Family is the real thing to discuss here. Not business. Bah! You know what big business brings? Big headaches, that's what."

"Now, Aurelia," Nikos started to say.

"She's right," Amy said.

Demetri looked at her sternly. "This is not a matter for children to be deciding."

Lisa sat straight up in her chair. "Now, wait a minute. I may not agree with Amy, but—"

"Enough!" Merrick's booming voice drew a tense silence from the small group. It also drew the attention of others up and down the beach, Amy noticed. Kieran had wandered back with her younger cousins in tow and stood peering at them from a distance. Nearby friends and neighbors paused, ears cocked in the direction of the Hardaway umbrellas. Merrick's words carried easily, cooperating with efforts to eavesdrop. "We're not going into this now. And we certainly don't need help making a decision that is ours alone to make.''

Demetri Costas raised his prominent nose a notch. ''I see. Our opinion—the opinion of all forty-one of us in the Costas family—is of no importance to the great Hardaway family. In that case—''

''Pop.'' Jon's voice broke in with such authority that Demetri grew quiet. ''Mr. Hardaway is right. Now isn't the time to discuss business.''

''But—''

''Come on, Pop. Let's go plan our strategy for the surf-fishing contest.''

''Surf fishing!'' Demetri waved a hand and turned to go. ''Jimmy, he can surf-fish. Hardaways, they can have things any way they please. Me, I am just a baker. What do I know?''

He stomped through the sand as best he could in rubber-soled sandals. Nikos shrugged and went after him. Leda spotted her grandchildren and shooed them away. Aurelia smiled apologetically at the Hardaways. ''Someday, somebody listens to Aurelia, and nobody makes himself the fool. Am I right?''

Then she trailed after her family without waiting for an answer.

Jon shook his head. ''Sorry. They get worked up.''

Amy watched her father bring his temper under control. ''No harm done.''

Jon stayed and made small talk with Megan and Lisa, asking them about their visit, being sociable.

His smile fell on Amy like a balm, until she realized
that no one else was reacting that way to his presence. Helene glared at him and began to twist her
earring. The crease in Megan's forehead deepened
and she stared pointedly at Amy. Lisa reached for
part of her father's paper, ignoring her ex-husband.
Only Merrick seemed oblivious to the tension.

No one invited him to stay. No one offered him
a chair or the corner of a beach blanket. Amy almost
spoke when he turned to go, hating to admit that she
dreaded being left alone with her family. She knew
her gaze followed his departure the way a pup followed a playmate. And once again she turned to find
Lisa's gaze trained on her. Not on Jon, but on her
sister.

Amy looked away.

"Well," Megan said, "at least that's over."


IT WASN'T OVER. Not by a long shot. Now that Demetri Costas had brought the Silver Sands offer out
in the open, everyone in town seemed compelled to
share an opinion with the Hardaways. And they all
seemed to want to do so before the holiday ended.

Some who came up to them that day thought they
should sell. Plenty thought they should be ashamed
to show their faces for even considering selling. A
few—very few—were open-minded enough to drop
by to ask questions about Silver Sands' plans before
making up their minds.

But whatever anyone in town thought, someone in the Hardaway family disagreed.

Jon watched the skirmishes from a distance. At least it was better than getting caught up in his own family's good-natured squabbling. What time to eat. Whose turn to run the bakery booth. Should Nikos wear a cap to keep the sun off the thinning spot on the top of his head. Whether the kids really had to wait an hour after eating to go back in the water. In the Costas family, all of it was up for grabs and everyone had the right to tell everyone else what to do and how to do it.

It was the kind of stuff that used to make him nuts. Today, for reasons he couldn't pin down, the petty quarreling didn't bother him. Maybe it was just the contrast with the Hardaways, all of whom seemed miserable on a day when the rest of the community was celebrating. Maybe it was the meeting in South Florida that awaited him on Tuesday, and the promise of rescue. Whatever the reason, today Jon could see that the bickering and controlling were done in the spirit of love, and in the end nobody remained angry with anyone else.

Jon knew the Hardaways well enough to know it didn't happen that way with them. An argument was an argument. Feelings were wounded. Wounds were nursed. In solitude. They didn't heal together, they went off alone and wounds became scars.

Jon considered the advantages of having a rowdy, close-knit family.

He watched when Amy and Lisa walked toward the pier together. He told himself to leave them alone. But he kept an eye on them, and when he saw them exchange angry words, he couldn't stop himself. He followed them.

By the time he reached the pier, Amy had disappeared. Lisa was pacing the pier, clearly oblivious that everyone else on the pier was strolling, enjoying the sunshine and festivities. He caught up with her at the end of the pier and fell in step beside her.

"This isn't turning into much of a visit," he said.

"I'm not looking for a sympathetic ear," she said.

"I know."

She paused at the end of the pier and put her hands atop a wooden piling, laying them flat, a gesture of composure. Jon remembered watching that outward composure many times when she needed a defense against some private inner turmoil.

Whatever Lisa guarded, it was deep and old and would take a better man than he to search it out.

"It's hard on Amy," he said, "seeing the family break up this way."

"The family isn't breaking up," Lisa said stiffly. "And at the risk of repeating myself, this really isn't any of your concern."

She turned to go and he put a hand on her arm. "I didn't know you were still so angry with me."

"I'm not—" She stopped abruptly, and the careful coolness dropped away from her expression.

"You turned my life upside down once. Don't do it again."

"I don't know what you're talking about." But he did, and he worried that his guilt showed.

"Stay away from Amy. She's sweet and naive and I don't want you luring her in before she knows what's going on."

Hadn't he thought the same things himself. "I'm a friend, that's all."

"Who are you kidding, Jon?"

Her gaze was sharp, pinning him with the question. He hesitated over the answer and she smiled knowingly.

Then she turned and marched back up the pier. Jon spotted Amy standing by a vendor's pushcart, staring at them. He started toward her, but before he could reach her she turned and fell into step with Lisa.

The urge to follow Amy swept over him. He needed to look into her eyes and feel the warm glow that always seemed to emanate from somewhere deep inside her. He needed to tell her about this yearning buried deep within him.

He wanted to tell her he...

He refused, once again, to name it.

He let her go. Maybe Lisa would warn her off and that would be that. He had other plans, anyway, didn't he? It was for the best.

KIERAN WAS SICK to death of the bickering and the loud kids and everybody pushing food on her. She hated this family stuff, she hated this barfy little town festival and she hated the feeling that she was the only one here who didn't fit in.

For that, she hated her father, who had left her here all alone.

She especially hated Jon, ever since overhearing him on the phone, arranging a job interview. Kieran's spirits had plummeted since then. She didn't want him to leave, she realized. What she really wanted was for him to put his arm around her and tell her she could depend on him, that he would always be there.

Right.

Kieran made her break after she and her aunt Christa put the youngest children down for an afternoon nap under one of the umbrellas. She started down the beach. Nobody would think anything of that. And soon she would be out of sight.

Hardball was asleep when she got there, sprawled out in the sun that beat down on the pier. She touched his shoulder and woke him, already excited by the prospect of having someone to talk to who understood her.

Someone besides Amy, she amended. In all fairness, she couldn't lump Amy in with the rest of them.

He jumped when he woke, an angry, defensive expression on his whiskery face. When he saw it was her, he said, "What the hell are you doing here?"

His tone wounded her, reminding her of the way her old man used to make her feel sometimes. Like everything was all her fault; like he wouldn't even do drugs if she weren't so dumb and incompetent. She looked down at her hands. "Sorry. I...I got sick of all the stupid games and stuff. I thought...I'm sorry."

He lifted her chin and looked contritely into her eyes. "Sorry, sunny bunny. I'm cranky when I first wake up."

She smiled and hoped that was it. But Kieran didn't like relying on her hopes. She also knew better than to make it worse by letting him see that her feelings were hurt. "No biggie."

"That's my girl. You bring anything to eat?"

She nodded and opened her vinyl backpack, which was crammed full of all the stuff she hadn't wanted herself. He smoked while she laid out her picnic, which he promptly devoured.

She waited until he had finished eating and sat back to light another cigarette, then said, "Tell me how you got so...free."

He inhaled deeply and held the smoke before letting it out in a pungent cloud. He passed the cigarette to her.

."We're all born that way," he said dreamily. "The question is, how'd you get so unfree."

"Wow." She passed the cigarette back to him

without taking a drag. "I never thought of it like that."

"'Course not. Most people don't. We live lives of quiet desperation."

She repeated his last two words reverently; they seemed to hold a secret she should have been able to see long before.

"You'll get the hang of it once we're on the road a while," he said. "You've got it in you to revert to the way we're really meant to be. I knew that the first time I read your stuff on the Net. Now, let's go over the plan again, so you don't get anything screwed up."

They reviewed the details. What time the bank opened on Monday and how quickly she could get out here after withdrawing their money. How long it would take them to get to the next town and what time the first bus rolled through on its way west.

"This time Monday night, we'll be long gone," Hardball said. "We'll be heading for bayou country. You ever been to New Orleans?"

She shook her head.

"Well, bunny, we might just make a stop in the Big Easy. Now, there's a town that could take you a long way toward gettin' free."

And he told her about the streetcars and the jazz clubs and the untold fortunes that could be made.

"First thing we're going to have to do is get you stoned, funny bunny," he said, holding the short butt of his cigarette under her nose until the acrid smoke snaked its way into her nostrils.

She wrinkled her nose and shook her head. "Is that what you're smoking?"

He just laughed and took another long draw. The stories resumed.

Uneasiness crept over Amy, the kind of uneasiness she hadn't felt in a while. It reminded her of the days when she'd known her old man was using. And once she'd made that connection, it was impossible not to make another connection, as well. Whenever her old man was using, he was always full of big plans, big dreams.

Just like Hardball.

But that was ridiculous. Hardball was nothing like her father. He wasn't a druggie like her father. These plans wouldn't come crashing down.

SOON, THE FIREWORKS would begin. But Amy had no enthusiasm for the promised display.

The rose-and-violet glow of sunset had finally faded, leaving the sky midnight dark. Watching the spectacular sunset, Amy had felt bittersweet at the knowledge that her day—her plans—would not draw to such a successful conclusion. She'd rested so many hopes on this week, on this day. And at its end, nothing had changed except her hopes. The fabric of her life still wore thin in spots, threatening to rend apart.

And she was apparently powerless to knit things together again.

Sitting back from her family, she watched each of them, pained by how separate they looked under their individual umbrellas. Merrick and Helene, one on either end of the blanket. Last year, as most every year she could remember since childhood, they'd drawn their chairs close together and held hands during the fireworks display.

Megan was chatting about her work, about the last book she'd read, about anything that would keep their focus off the dissension that had marked the early part of the day.

And, of course, Lisa, cool and aloof. Lisa, whom Jon had sought out earlier in the day. Her younger sister had behaved differently ever since. Very quiet, with an almost pensive expression on her face.

Disillusioned, Amy raised herself silently off the blanket and backed away from her family. Someone nearby turned on a boom box, tuning in the radio station that would broadcast Souza marches during the fireworks. Then another radio tuned in. Soon, the music would resound up and down the beach.

"Soon, Mama?" A child's excited voice carried from somewhere.

"Real soon, sweetheart."

Amy skirted the family groups and made her way down the beach, to the deserted gazebo near her house. She sat down to watch.

With the first thundering crack of the display, Jon

appeared. His presence didn't even startle her. And she knew as soon as she looked into his eyes that she wasn't going to ask him to leave. That she wasn't going to worry about what her mother would say. She smiled and he smiled back, a soft smile that reassured her.

He dropped down beside her, slipped his hand in hers and they watched the sky light up together.

# CHAPTER SIXTEEN

STARBURSTS OF COLOR and light erupted, and Amy felt the explosions in her soul. She felt warm inside, safe from life's blows.

The thunder of fireworks shuddered through her and she clutched Jon's hand. She couldn't—wouldn't—fight this any longer.

The sky became magic. And the magic touched Amy.

The heart of the little girl in her, the irrepressible part that always managed to hang on to another hope, another dream, leaped and laughed as a shower of light draped itself gracefully across the sky.

She looked at Jon, to see his reaction. But he was looking at her, not the fireworks. He smiled, a soft, gentle smile. And then he spoke, but his words were drowned by the next explosion. She saw the words his lips formed.

*I love you.*

Her heart seemed to halt for a moment. It couldn't be. Shouldn't be. She opened her mouth to tell him so, but another roll of thunder usurped her moment. Instead, she shook her head. Once. Twice.

In answer, he put his slender fingers on her chin and tilted her face to his.

Beneath the glittering sky, he kissed her and drew her into his arms. And it felt right. Amy's conscience vanished in the night, banished by the fireworks and the kiss and the words she'd seen him speak.

*I love you.*

LISA FELT GUILTY.

The day had gone badly and she felt responsible. Amy had tried so hard, had rested so much hope on this day. And Lisa had done nothing but make it worse. In part, at least, because no matter how hard she tried, some of her resented her sister's ability to look at life with childlike wonder.

Amy could still hope.

Lisa had hopes, too. After all, she had a new man in her life. But most of her hopes, she had to admit, she saved for the girls who came to the group home she ran. For them, it was not too late.

Or for Amy, either. The only problem Amy had, as Lisa saw it, was that she persisted in living in a dream world. A dreamworld in which Jon Costas was only a friend. A dreamworld in which grown women could turn back time and be sisters in innocence once again.

Still, she thought as she looked around at the empty spot on the blanket where Amy had sat most of the day, she felt guilty for not helping her sister along. Amy had done nothing wrong. Maybe it was time to reach out.

The first of the fireworks had just strewn sparkles of red and green across the cloudless sky when she stood and went in search of Amy. She thought she knew where to find her. In one of her many bursts of childlike enthusiasm during their walk home from Sea Haven the night before, Amy had pointed out the gazebo where she liked to go to be alone and paint or think.

She found the spot easily enough. And she was right. Amy had crept off. But not to be alone. Lisa's heart did a quickstep. Hidden in the shadows, her sister was wrapped in a man's embrace, her waterfall of wild curls giving away her identity. Lisa had a moment of envy for her sister.

Then another burst of fireworks exploded overhead, illuminating the couple, shedding just enough light to reveal the silvery glint of the man's hair.

It took a moment for what Lisa saw to sink in. The man kissing her sister was Jon. Her ex-husband. Hadn't she just warned him not to toy with Amy's affection? Lisa looked again. Amy certainly seemed to be a full participant. Her arms were tightly wound about Jon's neck, her eyes closed. Lisa smiled bitterly. The last thing she would have expected from naive, good-hearted Amy was this total lack of concern for her sister's emotions.

Betrayal, sharp and swift, pierced her, a feeling

so acute all she could do was run back to Amy's beach house and shut herself in the spare bedroom.

WHEN AMY TOOK Lisa to the airport the next morning—Megan opted to stay and visit with their mother—her sense of failure was complete.

Not only had Lisa disappeared the night before, bailing out on their promised discussion of the Silver Sands offer, she had offered no explanation this morning. In fact, Lisa seemed cooler and more withdrawn than ever, something Amy wouldn't have imagined possible. She barely had three words all the way to Tallahassee.

"What do you want me to tell Mom and Dad?" Amy asked, trying for a conversation one last time while waiting for boarding to begin.

"Whatever you think."

"But...you think they should sell."

"What goes on here doesn't concern me," Lisa said, her tone clipped and unemotional.

The boarding announcement crackled over the sound system. Amy was running out of time. She wanted to hug her sister. To burst into tears. Something, anything, to wrench some response out of her. "What about the anniversary celebration? I was thinking of something with a World War II theme. A USO party, maybe. Or we could do a vaudeville routine on their life. I can't sing, but you can. And Megan would make a great straight man—she never did laugh at all those corny jokes you used to collect. What do you think? You'll come back this summer, won't you?''

Lisa picked up her carry-on bag. ''I don't know.''

''You don't know!'' Amy knew the words came out as a wail, but she couldn't help it. Things were worse than ever and she couldn't figure out why. ''But, Lisa, it's family.''

''Family?'' Lisa gave her a look that for the first time had a hint of emotion in it. ''Like Jon? Is he family now, too?''

''I don't... What... But...'' Amy stammered, feeling her face grow warm, giving her away.

Lisa's smile was bitter. ''Have your fun, Amy. But don't come to me talking about family.''

She wheeled and walked toward the woman checking tickets. Amy followed her. ''Wait, Lisa. You don't...''

Lisa disappeared down the long corridor toward the plane. She didn't look back.

''...understand.''

Amy stared out the grimy window at the plane that would carry her sister back to Connecticut, wishing desperately she could do things differently, change the outcome. But it had played out just as she had feared. Lisa was hurt. Exactly as Amy had known she would be. Despair squeezed Amy's heart.

''I'm sorry,'' she whispered when the plane rolled away from the terminal.

All the way back to Hurricane Beach, Amy struggled with her emotions. What on earth had she done? How *could* she have committed such craziness? And how in the world did Lisa guess, when she'd gone out of her way to give Lisa and Jon a chance to be together, to see what they'd lost?

Obviously, for Jon at least, all her efforts had been futile. Hadn't he followed her last night? Kissed her? Whispered words in her ear that frightened her. Love? How could he love her? And didn't Lisa's reaction prove that her sister still felt something for him?

Or did it simply prove what Amy had known deep down all along, that falling for your sister's ex-husband wasn't acceptable behavior.

*You haven't fallen for him,* she told herself one more time as she turned off the main highway to the narrow two-lane that paralleled Alligator Creek on its winding route to Hurricane Beach. But her protest rang awfully hollow. Amy knew that she no longer had that much denial in her. She had fallen in love with Jon. She'd known it long before he said the words the night before.

It was only the fear of the consequences that had kept her silent, that had kept her from admitting the truth even to herself. And now, the consequences had come despite her efforts.

She drove up to Sea Haven, for the first time in her life dreading a meeting with her family.

Helene and Megan were on the deck, sipping lemonade and reading. The sight of them, each in her own little world, snapped something in Amy's heart. She knew that no matter how much she loved them, no matter how much she would always love them, she needed more.

She knew where to get it, too.

"Lisa's safely off," she said, pouring a glass of lemonade for herself from the pitcher on the table. Her hand trembled slightly.

"What happened to her last night?" Helene asked, looking up from her book. "She just disappeared."

"You both disappeared," Megan said pointedly, and Amy knew she needn't pretend any longer. She wanted it all out in the open.

"She's angry with me," Amy said. She took a long swallow of lemonade for courage. "Because she knows I'm...in love with Jon."

There. She'd said it. She couldn't believe how light her heart felt now that it was no longer burdened with the secret.

"Oh, Amy, no!" Helene slammed her book shut. "You promised!"

"I don't believe this," Megan said, clearly stunned.

"Believe it," Amy said, suddenly strong in her convictions. "I didn't intend for it to happen, but it has and everybody is just going to have to deal with it."

"Well, that's hardly the attitude I would have expected from you," Helene said. "I suppose poor Lisa is brokenhearted."

"Mom, they've been divorced forever," Amy said.

"Lisa did leave Jon," Megan conceded.

"Still and all," Helene said, "I'm not going to allow something like this to destroy our family. You and that young man will just have to...to...contain yourselves."

Amy set her glass on the table. "Mom, I don't see how this can possibly make things any worse than they already are. Look at us. We never talk to each other. We dance around the things that hurt us instead of bringing them out in the open. We aren't close anymore. It breaks my heart to say it, but it's true. But I can be close to Jon. And I intend to."

"Over my dead body," Helene said.

"Now, Mom," Megan said, reaching out to put a calming hand on their mother's arm.

"I mean it! I won't stand for this!"

Amy drew a deep breath and said, "I'm not asking permission, Mom. I'm a grown-up. And the only one whose happiness I'm responsible for anymore is mine. I hope you'll learn to accept that."

Helene's only reaction was the cold displeasure in her eyes. Amy walked out, needing to get out of the house before the tears fell. They blurred her eyes and she ran squarely into her father. He encircled her with his arms.

"Oh, Dad," she said, burying her face in his chest.

He hugged her tightly. "I know. I heard everything. I'm proud of you, Amy Serena. It shall all turn out. You'll see."

"Proud of me? How can you be proud of me?"

He put a finger under her chin and raised her face, looking into her eyes. His smile was as warm as it had ever been. "Because you spoke out. Because you know your heart. That's courage, Amy."

"Then why do I feel so scared?" she whispered, once again pressing her damp cheek to her father's chest.

SHE CALLED LISA that night, but the ever-present machine was all she got on the other end of the line. She waited for the beep and said, "I'm sorry this has hurt you. I never intended that, and neither did Jon. I love you, but I love him, too. I hope one day you can accept that."

Then she hung up. In her mind's eye she could see her sister listening, stone-faced, to her call, determined not to discuss the situation with Amy.

"Oh, Sam, what am I going to do?"

The big dog suggested a nap.

"If I napped every time I ran into a conflict, where would the world be today? Who'd keep things on their axis?"

"Talking to yourself is supposed to be a bad sign."

She whirled, the ache in her heart dissipating for the first time that day. "Jon."

He slid the screen door open and came in.

"I wasn't," she said. "I was talking to Sam. I just don't get much response, that's all." She chuckled wryly. "From anyone."

"I'll talk to you," he said, taking her by the hand and pulling her onto the love seat with him. "When everyone else abandons you, you can count on me."

She tried to keep it light and impersonal, although her heart cried out to unburden itself. "And if you're the reason everyone's abandoning me?"

He nodded. "Ah. Lisa."

"She knows."

"What exactly does everyone know?"

Amy felt her cheeks grow warm. After all, what had happened in the dark of night, muffled by the boom of fireworks, hadn't yet been brought into the open.

"I want to hear it from you, Amy. What is there to know?"

"About...us."

"That I love you?"

Hearing the words aloud gave her courage.

"That I love you," Amy said. "I've told them all."

There it was. Love. The thing she didn't want to believe but couldn't deny. She'd felt it the instant she'd heard his voice, that lightening of spirit that said everything would now be all right. Because Jon had come.

Love, the cause of the problem. And the solution.

He kissed her then. Soft and gentle, with only a little hunger to give it an edge. Amy yielded completely to the kiss, no longer constrained by her fears that this was wrong, something to hide. She allowed herself the luxury of not fighting the feel of his warm lips on hers, the damp tip of his tongue exploring the curve of her upper lip.

Yes, she wanted Jon. It could be that simple, couldn't it?

Cradled in his arms, she allowed his kisses to lull her, acquiesced when his tentative caresses grew more intimate. He coaxed and she surrendered. His kisses trailed along her neck, following the path laid bare when her silk shirt slipped off her shoulder. His hand traced the slope of her back, the inward curve of her waist. And his long, hard thigh molded itself to hers.

She wanted the promise his body made to hers and she was ready to let the future take care of itself.

She looked into his eyes and took his face between her hands. It felt lean and hard, but his dark eyes were soft and full. She kissed him, pressing herself to him, trying to ease the ache in her breasts with nearness. But nearness wasn't enough. She unbuttoned his shirt, felt the electric shock of his warm flesh against her palm. His chest was lush with thick, dark hair. His nipples pebbled against her palm. He groaned. She sighed.

She cast off her top, and with it the camisole that covered her small breasts. And for one split second she wondered if he was comparing her, if he was thinking of someone else. Then she saw the absorption in his eyes and knew that yesterday's lovers mattered no more for him than they did for her.

While she fumbled with his clothing, he brushed his hands up her outer thighs. He slipped one hand inside the loose-fitting tap pants she wore, and she gasped at the fire in his touch. He massaged and probed and brought her to hot, wet readiness. Then she settled over his lap, her full skirt covering them, and pulled him into her one aching inch at a time.

They moved together, eyes locked in as intimate an embrace as the rest of their bodies.

When it was over—when he had cried out and clutched her hips tightly to his and spilled into her, hot and fast, and she had shuddered in taking him into her—she knew that yesterday no longer mattered.

What mattered were all the tomorrows.

## CHAPTER SEVENTEEN

SAM GAVE UP the hammock, turning it over to Amy and Jon so they could rock gently under the gathering clouds and listen to the steady rush of breaking waves.

"I can't get enough of this," Jon said, sweeping his free arm to indicate their surroundings. His other arm cradled Amy against his side. "I can't get enough of you."

He'd already astounded her by confessing how long ago he'd first yearned for her. Amy, sure that dreams were at long last coming true, had shared her own adolescent fantasies. She'd never felt so right, so perfectly right, anywhere.

"You said that before, about how perfect it is here," she said drowsily. "I've thought about it a lot since then, about how right it feels to be here in Hurricane Beach, just listening, watching."

"Smelling," he added. "I like the salt in the air. None of those sissy sweet smells, like magnolia and mimosa. Give me some real-world smells right down on the docks when Jimmy's boats come in."

Amy laughed. "Mimosa and magnolia are real-world, too. So are cinnamon and yeast, don't forget."

"Maybe."

He grew quiet for the first time in a while and Amy sensed something uncomfortable in his silence. "You're still not happy at the bakery."

"It's okay. I don't expect to be there long."

"You don't?"

He shifted, then waited for the hammock to still itself again. Amy wondered if he was stalling.

"Actually, I've been meaning to tell you. I have an interview."

An alarm sounded in her heart. "An interview?"

"For a job. Day after tomorrow."

"Oh." Amy's heart constricted. He wasn't exactly rushing forward to fill her in on the details. "Want to tell me about it?"

"Sure, sure."

Haltingly, he told her about a man he'd worked with in New York who owned an international chain of hotels and resorts. The man who wanted to establish headquarters in South Florida, and wanted Jon to come down and handle finances for him. As Amy listened, Jon sounded farther away with each word he spoke.

"It's like a dream come true for me," he said. "Getting out of New York, but not being tied down here."

"What about Kieran?"

Because she couldn't ask the questions that had come to her first. *What about me? What about us?*

He was silent again. Amy felt the ache starting slowly in her heart.

"Kieran will be fine. I think she's turned a corner, don't you?"

Amy thought the girl didn't need to be abandoned again, but for once in her life she kept quiet.

"Besides, Kieran can come with me. With us."

"With us?" The way he'd said it sounded like an afterthought.

"Sure. I thought, I mean, doesn't this seem like the perfect way to start fresh? No baggage."

Amy sat upright on the hammock. "I don't want to start fresh."

"Why not?"

"This is my home, Jon. This is where my family is. My business. I can't just walk away."

"But everything's turned upside down with your family. It might make it easier to smooth things over with a little distance between you."

She slid off the hammock and looked down at him. His eyes pleaded with her to understand. "Walking away never works, Jon. It didn't work for Lisa or Megan. It hasn't even worked for you, but here you are wanting to try it all over again. Well, I won't do that."

"Then you won't come with me?"

"Then you won't stay here with me?" she countered.

"Amy, you don't understand. An opportunity like this—"

"That's money, Jon. I thought you understood there are things more important than money."

"Well, of course, but..." His protest faded out. She saw the apology in his eyes. "Amy, I have to do this. It's what I've had in mind for a long time now. Please tell me you'll come with me."

Amy remembered the shock and disappointment in her mother's eyes when she'd said she loved Jon Costas. She remembered the hurt in Lisa's eyes before she boarded the plane. She hadn't regretted the risks she'd taken, because she did love Jon Costas and she believed he loved her.

She still believed in that love.

But she'd already given up plenty for the sake of it. Her family's trust and approval, the chance for renewing her relationship with her sister. Could she really give up more? Her business, her best friend, her home?

"I can't tell you that, Jon."

And she wasn't willing to ask again for him to abandon his dreams. That was no more fair than what he was asking of her, it seemed.

"What happens, then?" he asked.

"You go to South Florida on Tuesday."

When he walked away a few minutes later, she wanted to wish him good luck. But she didn't have it in her heart.

THE BIG CELEBRATION was over, but things hadn't calmed down in Hurricane Beach by Monday morning.

Everybody in town continued to buzz about the possibility of the Silver Sands development. Despite the continuous drizzle that was not quite warm, not quite chilly, a steady stream of visitors came by Rêve Rags to talk about the plan.

Amy had no interest in discussing the future. Whatever happened, she supposed she would weather it. All she wanted was to nurse her wounds. She wanted to forget that she'd sabotaged her relationship with her family for the sake of a man who was now going to walk away.

On a day when she ought to be feeling euphoric, still bathed in a certain afterglow, she remembered waking up alone and lonely. So she'd walked to work restless, irritable and discontented, wishing for nothing more than to be left alone.

A wish, it seemed to Amy, that was certain to be granted.

JON STOOD in the kitchen doorway, only vaguely aware of the heated discussions about Silver Sands Development and the Hardaway clan.

*After all,* came the biting little voice in his head, *what happens in Hurricane Beach doesn't matter to you. You're bailing out on everybody who needs you. Again.*

The accusations rang loud and clear in his mind,

but strangely enough they did nothing to mask the other things that weighed so heavily on his mind.

Things like the silken texture of Amy Hardaway's skin. The lushness of her hair draped over his chest. The faraway softness that came into her piercing green eyes during moments of passion. The way her breathy voice grew even more breathy.

And, of course, the way she'd retreated to that place where grown-up problems like career didn't intrude. Her own personal little Never-never land.

And, of course, there was Kieran, too. Damn, but he wanted to make things right for her. He wanted to be everything she needed. He felt guilty about his niece. He'd tried telling himself he wasn't her father. That others were better equipped to deal with her. That Nick ought to be the one to come back.

But that didn't make his heart hurt any less when he thought of her. And it didn't make the guilt go away, either.

So he thought of Kieran. He thought of Amy. And a part of him couldn't wait to get out of Hurricane Beach so he could begin forgetting.

But the bottom line was, even with the prospect of his dream job waiting on tomorrow's horizon, Jon felt empty. And no amount of debate over the pros and cons of building condos and golf courses at Hurricane Beach made a damn bit of difference to him.

"I don't suppose it matters much what we think," he said. "The Hardaways will decide what they want and the rest of us will have to make the best of it."

No one liked the idea that the Hardaways would decide their fate. Another buzz started. Jon was grateful when the phone rang, giving him a chance to escape.

"Costas Family Bakery."

A stern male voice said, "I'd like to speak with the guardian responsible for Kieran Costas, please."

Jon stiffened. "This is Jon Costas, her uncle."

"Mr. Costas, this is Vice Principal Donald Bolling over at the junior high. It's come to my attention that your niece isn't in school today."

Jon's stomach clenched a little more tightly. "I see."

"Now, normally this wouldn't require a call, but we've had a bit of trouble with your niece this year and, well, it seems this absence puts her in danger of missing more days of school than the law allows."

And Jon had thought things were going better since Kieran had started working for Amy. He sighed and was about to assure Mr. Bolling he would be in with Kieran first thing the next morning to straighten things out. Then he remembered his job interview. Someone else—his mother, he supposed—would have to fill in for him.

*The way you're filling in for Nick. What a lucky niece you have.*

As he finished the arrangements and hung up, the

buzz in the front of the bakery drew to an abrupt halt with the tinkling of the bell over the door. He peered out to see Amy Hardaway looking around her uncertainly. When she saw Jon, embarrassment flickered across her face for an instant.

"Jon, is there some reason Kieran didn't come to work today?"

Before he could answer, the branch manager from First City Bank set the front bell ajangle again. Hildegarde Pretz seemed taken aback by the silence and the dozen sets of eyes that turned on her. But when she spotted Jon, she collected herself and said, "Mr. Costas, are you aware that your niece has closed out her bank account?"

Her bank account? That was news to Jon.

"Do you suppose we could discuss this in private?" the bank manager said, lowering her voice. "There appears to be some irregularities that we need to discuss with your niece."

NEWS OF THE disappearance of Kieran Costas turned the town on its ear. More than one person, including each one of the Hardaways, remembered the last time a child had disappeared in Hurricane Beach. Most upset of all was Megan, who remembered the stranger she'd seen arrive in town, and her reluctance to mention him to anyone, for fear of seeming paranoid.

Some of that anguish eased when word also made the rounds that Kieran Costas probably wasn't some innocent victim of foul play. In fact, she had taken a considerable sum of money with her—money she had pilfered from merchants all over town using the computer at Rêve Rags.

Nevertheless, the entire town pulled together to find the missing teenager.

"I don't care what anyone says," Glenda Hendricks, the boutique owner, said. "Since she's been working for Amy, I've had the chance to get to know her a little bit and I don't think she meant any harm, whatever she's done."

"I agree," said Dale Griffen who owned the dry cleaning store on Gulfview. "She's troubled, that's all."

Old man Thompson, the pharmacist, nodded his balding head. "Given all that's happened, anybody could understand that."

A few eyes strayed to Grace then, and to the stricken faces of Leda and Demetri Costas.

So the people of Hurricane Beach began to fan out in all directions, eyes peeled for any sign of the missing girl. Most of the shops closed for the day. Expressions turned grimly determined, as if will-power alone could avert a tragedy.

Even Helene and Merrick went out—together— to scour their sprawling acreage in search of the teenager.

There was only one person whose help Jon really wanted. He needed Amy, because he'd never felt the kind of fear he felt right now, thinking of his young niece out there somewhere, alone and vulnerable. He could talk to Amy about his fears in a way he couldn't talk to anyone else.

But he couldn't ask for that kind of help, because he'd made it clear the night before that he wasn't willing to commit wholeheartedly, unless she did things his way.

After the chief of police organized search parties and a group to stay by the phones, Jon headed for the docks. He'd reached the end of Gulfview and stepped off into the sand, when he heard a voice. Amy's voice. He told himself it was only in his imagination. Still, when he heard it a second time, he turned. Amy ran to catch up with him.

"Let me go with you," she said.

He longed to have her with him. Just hearing her offer filled his heart.

"I'm going out with Jimmy." He gestured toward his cousin's boat. "In case. With a kid, you never know."

Amy shuddered, and not, he suspected, from the rain, which had grown colder as the afternoon wore on. He prayed that Kieran hadn't taken off into the Gulf of Mexico, especially in this weather. The water was choppy, whitecaps furling menacingly on its surface. But Kieran was just impulsive enough to have done exactly that.

"I'm coming with you," she said.

"You don't need to do that," he said, but he hoped she would.

"Yes, I do."

More grateful than he knew how to say at the moment, he took her by the hand and they boarded the boat together. Jimmy acknowledged Amy's presence with a grim-faced nod, tossed each of them one of the rain suits his crew wore in bad weather and pointed the boat into the rough waters.

Jon's heart thumped in rough time with the noisy chug of the engine as it fought each cresting wave. He scanned the horizon, wiping the water from his eyes as the rain picked up in intensity. He imagined all that might have happened to his niece.

"It'll turn out okay," Amy said. "I just know it will."

He looked at her. "Thanks for being here."

"Jon…"

"I bought Kieran a puppy once," he said, the memories crowding in, painful and poignant. "For her fifth birthday. Nick didn't like it, didn't want the bother. But she was thrilled. She was missing a front tooth and she hadn't wanted to smile for weeks. But when I brought that puppy in—"

He couldn't go on. He couldn't voice the other memories. The day she was born. The crayon-and-construction-paper birthday card she'd sent him one year. And, of course, the belligerent way she'd looked at him every time he'd tried to talk to her this last month.

"This is my fault," he said.

"Don't say that. You couldn't have known."

"I held out on her." He saw in Amy's face that she knew what he meant, and he wondered if Kieran had ever said anything to Amy. Amy made it so easy for everyone to open up. "I wouldn't commit. I made sure everyone knew I wouldn't be around forever. And...I can see now that was wrong. I can see now she needed to know that I, at least, wouldn't bail out on her."

Amy opened her mouth as if to speak, then closed it abruptly and lowered her eyes.

"I can see now," Jon said, taking her hand in his, "I was wrong. She deserved to know I would be there for her, as long as she needed me."

They sat in silence and turned searching gazes back to the water.

"I keep thinking I should be able to come up with some ideas," Amy said. "I keep thinking I knew her better than anyone, that if I just think hard enough I'll remember something."

"I'm her guardian. I'm supposed to protect her. Great job I've done."

"You didn't create this problem," Amy said. "Things were worse before you got involved in her life. Remember?"

"No, things were worse before *you* got involved. That's what I remember."

They rode the rough waters, hoping for a sign of the flare that would signal someone in town had found Kieran. The rain pounded them now, chilling them to the bone. And the sun was almost gone for the day. But they saw no flare and they saw no sign of a teenager in any kind of craft. They went west first, far past Alligator Bay and beyond, then doubled back and headed east.

It was sometime after that, after they'd bypassed town, after they'd bypassed the stretch of beach where a dark and empty-looking Sea Haven perched atop a slight incline, that Amy clutched his arm and pointed toward shore.

"The old pier! Jon, she told me once that's where she always goes when she wants to get away from…things."

Things like her uncle, he supposed.

Jimmy maneuvered the boat as close to the pier as possible. The structure looked ready to cave in, Jon thought, and the old shack on one end couldn't have been keeping anyone very dry on a day like today. As Jon lassoed the end piling, Amy reached for the opposite piling.

"No," Jon said, putting a restraining hand on her. This wasn't hers to fix. It was his. "I'll go. This is my responsibility."

"I want to go."

"Why?"

Amy looked up at him and said, "Because I think she trusts me."

The words stabbed him, but he couldn't deny their accuracy. He gave her a boost and she walked down the pier, stepping over places where the wood had rotted through. Her wet hair was plastered to her back and she looked fragile in the pelting rain. Jon's heart was full and tormented and still fearful as he watched her go.

KIERAN WAS COLD and damp huddled in the small, leaky room. She was becoming disillusioned, also, although she wasn't ready to admit that.

Hardball hadn't wanted to go in the rain. Tomorrow would be fine, he'd insisted, although hanging around all day had Kieran worrying what would happen once everybody discovered she was gone. Especially if they discovered the bank account she'd closed that morning, and where she'd gotten the money for it in the first place.

But Hardball wasn't worried.

"You wouldn't be, either, if you'd loosen up a little," he'd said.

Then he'd offered her his half-smoked cigarette and Kieran thought about how naive she'd been. She knew the cigarettes he smoked continuously weren't tobacco at all. She felt uneasy about that. But it was too late to turn back. Too late to do anything but keep going.

She wondered if that's how her old man felt sometimes.

Kieran had thought about her father a lot these last few days. Since Hardball had arrived, she told herself. Although there was no real connection there.

Sundown was only moments away, and the day had already turned gray and dark. She couldn't imagine waiting out the night here, getting colder and wetter. The rain poured down now. Kieran heard it, watched it slanting toward the ground through the tiny broken window. The ugly weather frightened her. She felt unprotected, vulnerable to all kinds of threats from the world.

She wouldn't have admitted it for all the money in the world, but right now she was thinking longingly of her bedroom at home, of the quilt folded at the foot of her bed and the window that kept out the rain and the cold on days like this. From her room, she could watch the wind in the trees and know she didn't have to feel any of it. But this was the real world, a place where no one—not even Hardball— was really there for her, to keep the rain off her.

Her own father wasn't there for her; what made her think Hardball would be?

He was sleeping now. Snoring. She thought about running home, but it was too late. She didn't have the money any longer. She'd given it to Hardball and she couldn't go back empty-handed. It was too late.

The door creaked, opened. Kieran's heart leaped in her chest. Someone rushed in out of the rain. Amy.

"Thank God!" Amy dropped to the floor beside her, rain streaming down her face. "Are you all right?"

"Of course." Kieran tried to sound grown-up,

confident, even a little defensive at being followed, tracked down like an unruly kid.

The truth was, she was so glad to see Amy. She wanted to throw herself into Amy's arms. But she didn't.

"I hope you're ready to come home," Amy said matter-of-factly. "Because I'm freezing my behind off."

Kieran hesitated, wondering if Amy knew the extent of her betrayal. "I don't know…"

Hardball stirred, gazed at the two of them through half-closed eyes. "What's this? The posse?"

"She's a friend."

"A friend, huh? Be careful who you call your friend, sunny bunny."

"She is!"

"And who are you?" Amy said. Her voice held none of the judgmental scorn Kieran might have expected from an adult. But Kieran also noticed it didn't hold any of Amy's usual friendliness, either.

"Me, I'm a friend. A real friend. A true friend. Am I right, money bunny?"

The reference to the money embarrassed Kieran. "Cut it out."

"Did he touch you?" Amy said.

Hardball laughed. "Not yet. There's a lot of demand out there for fresh fruit, you know."

His words made Kieran uneasy, although she didn't believe he meant what he seemed to be saying. He was saying it to shock Amy, that was all.

Before Amy could react, he took out one of his marijuana cigarettes and lit it, taking a long drag and blowing the smoke in Amy's direction.

Now Amy *did* look scornful. She turned to Kieran and said, "He's trouble, Kieran. You can do better. Why don't you come home with me."

Hardball laughed again.

Kieran wanted nothing more than to do what Amy suggested. But her conscience whispered at her, *Too late.* She hung her head and said softly, "They'll throw me in jail."

Amy put a hand on her shoulder. "We'll straighten it out. Everybody's going to be so glad to see you back, I promise you it'll work out."

"Oh, that's a good one," Hardball said on a sneer. "I'll bet the whole town's out looking for its favorite lost daughter."

"As a matter of fact, they are."

Kieran looked at Amy for confirmation. She tried to imagine the people of Hurricane Beach caring that much. Another image came to mind instead. "I'll bet Uncle Jon's really hot."

"He's scared. Just like the rest of us."

"Scared?"

"He loves you."

Kieran looked at Amy, expectantly, hopefully.

"Don't be a dumb bunny," Hardball said.

"I love you, too," Amy said.

Kieran threw herself into Amy's arms. "Can we go home now?"

# CHAPTER EIGHTEEN

JON HAD NEVER been so grateful as when he saw
Amy emerge with her arm around his niece's narrow, sagging shoulders.

He helped them back onto the boat and wrapped
each of them in a slicker, his hands lingering on
Amy's shoulders.

"Thank you," he said, wanting to kiss her, wanting to taste the rain and saltwater on her cheeks.

"I don't need thanking," she said softly. Her eyes
strayed to Kieran, who huddled in the stern of the
boat with her knees clutched tightly under her chin.

Jon understood her unspoken message. Amy
might or might not need him at the moment, but
Kieran definitely did. Kieran needed his reassurance
and he gave it to her. He sat beside her, pulling her
against his side and securing her with the curve of
his arm. She held herself rigid at first, but it didn't
take long before she huddled against him.

"I'm glad you're safe," he said.

She remained silent, but he sensed the vigilance
in her tense body. She was waiting for recrimina-
tions.

"I'm glad you trusted Amy," he said. "You pick pretty good friends."

"Not all the time," she mumbled.

"Oh, well, if you're worried about *all* the time. You know, I never have figured out a way to get it right *all* the time." He felt her listless shrug. "Did I ever tell you about the time I decided to join an oil rig in New Orleans?"

She shook her head.

"I was fourteen."

She glanced up at him.

"It seemed like a good idea at the time. If Uncle Nikos hadn't come after me, I don't know where I would have ended up."

"Wow. I'm surprised you're not still grounded."

He chuckled. "Yeah. Me, too."

The memory itself surprised him, in fact. He hadn't thought of the incident in years. It had never occurred to him, until now, how lucky he'd been to have a smothering, busybody family looking out for him. His heart swelled with gratitude—and not just for having been rescued then. But for being able to see his family differently now than he'd been able to a few short months ago. "But I suppose I had to pull something pretty dumb or I never would have figured out how dumb it was. I mean, I wouldn't have believed anybody else if they'd told me."

Kind of like now, he thought ruefully.

Kieran's teeth were beginning to chatter and he

slipped off his slicker and added it to the one she already wore.

"I guess you were a perfect son after that."

"No. Just a little less dumb than I'd been before."

Kieran laughed a little and Jon thought things might just turn out all right. *Glad I could be here for this one, Nick.*

As Jimmy Costas chugged into Alligator Bay, a cheer went up from the people of Hurricane Beach.

Having seen the flare Jimmy set off when Amy and Kieran walked out of the shack at the old abandoned pier, all the searchers and all the worriers had gathered to welcome the boat. They cheered and they wrapped everyone who'd been on board in blankets and hugs and in the comfort that only a community of families can offer.

The spirit at the marina warmed Jon and, from the look on her face, it touched and surprised Kieran, as well.

Jon allowed himself to be swept up in the warmth of his hometown. He accepted the outpouring of love and relief and allowed it to touch something deep inside him. And as it did, he felt the unpleasant tug of his plans for the future.

He looked around and saw Kieran talking, eyes downcast, to Hildegarde Pretz, the bank manager, who looked concerned and magnanimous all at once, patting the girl's shoulder. He looked around and saw Jimmy recounting the rescue tale to a small group of searchers.

He saw Nikos, too, standing on the sidelines watching his nephew with a satisfied smile. Jon returned the smile and walked over to his uncle.

"You were right," Jon said.

Nikos just kept smiling.

"I do have more here than I ever dreamed."

Nikos's smile deepened and he put a hand on Jon's shoulder. "Good."

And that was all either of them needed to say. They understood all that had happened, all that had changed, without saying more.

Another benefit of family, Jon thought.

Then he saw the one he'd been looking for. Amy. Surrounded by her mother, her father, her sister Megan, who looked drawn and pale, and Grace. He started toward her, then Aurelia caught him by the arm. His mother took him by the other.

"Come, we have hot soup in the bakery," Aurelia said. "The family should be together."

"Okay, but—" He looked around for Amy and saw her drying her hair with one of the big, fluffy towels bearing the marina logo. He wanted her beside him, but he knew he had no right to ask that of her.

Not yet.

AMY HAD FELT ADRIFT when the boat docked at Alligator Bay. Everyone else had rushed together like family and she'd had no family to turn to.

She coveted the closeness she saw around her.

She realized she'd been using every trick in her bag to accomplish that for years, and nothing had worked. Even the good relationship she'd had with her parents lay in shambles now.

She didn't even have Jon any longer, unless she had the courage to accept his promise of a new family, a new beginning.

Did she have enough courage to leave behind the little-girl dreams she'd clung to for so long?

Could she release her own family with love and hope? Whether they loved her back was out of her hands now. Had been all along, she supposed. The notion she could control them was nothing more than illusion, she realized.

She took the big, soft towel someone offered and began blotting her tangled hair. But before she could reach any decisions, she was wrapped in a big hug she would have known anywhere—her dad's.

"Oh, Amy, we were so worried about you," Helene said. "I told Merrick as soon as we saw the flare that we had to hurry back."

"I told her you'd be fine." Merrick gave her one more squeeze before relinquishing her to her mother's embrace.

Even Megan's distress seemed to have diminished when she touched Amy's shoulder and said, "Might've known you'd be the hero of the hour."

Amy smiled, her love for them strong. "I love you all."

"Oh, darling, we love you, too," Helene said,

picking up the trailing end of the towel and blotting a stream of rainwater that trickled down Amy's cheek. "Nothing can change that."

"More than we know how to show sometimes," Merrick said solemnly.

Megan put a tentative hand on her sister's arm. "You do what you have to, Amy. Lisa will come around."

Amy was grateful for her sister's support. But she saw the distance that still lingered between her parents and wasn't sure anything could repair the places where her family was being torn apart.

AMY REACHED her cottage just as the phone began to ring. Sam stood impatiently at the door, demanding to be petted. The rain had stopped, but her damp clothes still clung uncomfortably to her clammy skin.

She debated answering the phone versus changing into dry clothes. Dry clothes won.

She felt better once she'd had a hot shower and swaddled herself in a pair of old sweats and two pairs of socks. Despite her pain over Jon's leaving, she felt a measure of peace she hadn't felt in months. Maybe years.

The phone rang again as she was opening a can of chicken soup and dumping it into a microwave bowl. The phone was still ringing as she punched in the time on the oven, so she answered.

"Lisa, what a surprise."

"Yes. Well...you sound strange."

Strange. Little wonder. "Strange? No, I'm fine. That is, Kieran ran away. But we found her. She's fine."

"Good."

Then it struck her. In her self-absorption, she hadn't noticed that Lisa was the one who really sounded strange. She gained a tiny bit of confidence. "You got my message."

"Yes."

"I might have spoken too soon. I think Jon's leaving Hurricane Beach."

"You'll go with him."

"No. I doubt it." But even as she said it, some part of Amy wondered if she could remain behind if he truly wanted her with him. "This is my home."

"Amy, don't cling too long to the past."

She didn't have an answer to that, so she simply said, "I never wanted to hurt you."

Amy heard her sister's deep sigh.

"I don't love him," Lisa said. "I haven't loved him for a long time. Sometimes I think back and I'm not sure I ever really loved him. But I can't promise that I'll ever be able to accept...this."

"But, Lisa..." Her voice cracked and she had to pause. "Y-you'll always be my sister. No matter what."

"I know." Lisa's reply was a soft, unconvincing whisper. "But maybe we—you—need to accept the fact it'll never be the way it was, Amy."

Amy listened to the dial tone and felt a void in her heart as Lisa's words sank in. If Lisa was right, Amy had struck her family a fatal blow. How could she live with that?

LISA SAT at her desk in her darkened office after she hung up, staring at the framed photograph on the corner of her desk. It was a faded Polaroid she'd had blown up and enhanced and she told herself she kept it here to remind herself what it was supposed to be like for the young girls she counseled, before their lives got offtrack.

But with Amy's voice still whispering in her ear, she wondered if that wasn't a weak rationalization.

In the picture, the three Hardaway sisters sat on a big inner tube, Megan in the middle, Lisa perched on one side, Amy draped across the front like a silent-movie vamp. Amy, always the dramatic one. They'd been so happy then, caught on the cusp of adolescence, their eyes alight with discovery and excitement and that naive sense that they would always live happily ever after.

None of them had. She wondered if Amy would somehow manage it now, given the baggage in the budding relationship between her and Jon.

She smiled faintly. Depend on Amy to jump into the middle of a situation normal people only encountered in soap operas. Odd, she should have realized long ago that Amy made a better choice for Jon than she had ever been. They complemented each other, filled in the chinks in each other. Jon so solid, Amy so sparkling. Like Merrick and Helene.

She wondered if a little more time together would prove that she and Patrick Dannon complemented each other in that same way. If not, she supposed, she would get by. After all, she'd learned at sixteen how to be a survivor.

She hoped Amy wouldn't have to get by any longer, that she would be happy. Jon, as well.

She should've said that to Amy, she knew. But she couldn't, somehow. Because a part of her held just a small touch of envy that things might work out so perfectly for bright, sparkling, talented, touched-by-magic Amy.

"Well," she said, turning the photo facedown and blinking back the tears that had suddenly filled her eyes. She clicked off her desk lamp, "I have a good life. I'm useful and productive and in control. Who needs magic?"

THE SLIDING DOOR onto the balcony was open in Helene's room.

So was her suitcase.

The ocean was restless tonight, tossing back and forth, back and forth, going nowhere but definitely disturbed.

So was Helene.

This charade she had instigated was no longer a charade. The fracture in her relationship with Merrick was painful and deep, and had revealed old wounds she'd never been aware of before now. Had clutched her so that she'd even begun taking things out on her own daughter.

*I should go,* she told herself. *Have it over with.*

She turned to her dresser, opened the top drawer. The glint of the gold-framed photograph on the dresser caught her eye, stilled the hand lingering over the silky items in her drawer. Merrick, a much younger Merrick, sat on the carousel in Panama City, surrounded by three little girls, all with golden hair and gap-toothed grins.

The four of them had been her whole life.

*How can I walk out on that?*

She swallowed back tears. *How can I not?*

AMY WAS IN BED, but not asleep.

He was leaving. She'd heard it from Kieran, who said he'd called from West Palm to say he'd taken the job. Jon Costas was leaving, and Amy couldn't find the courage to go with him.

Assuming he would even ask her again, which didn't seem likely.

Amy lay in bed and tried to tell herself that her life had been empty of men before and she'd managed just fine. But the admonition wasn't working. Because Jon wasn't just a man. He filled part of her that had been hollow for so long, the part of her that longed for someone to share with, dream with, laugh with.

She also knew that no one, man or woman, was

meant to go through life empty of those intimacies of the heart that Jon had brought into her life. She'd spent so many years looking for them, and to give them up now was far more bitter than never having experienced them.

She wanted to cry, but she was too empty, even for that.

The knock on her door came at half-past midnight. Amy's heart leaped.

"I suppose we have to get up and check," she said to Sam, who stirred and whimpered from his spot in front of her bedroom door. She tried not to sound excited, hopeful. A visitor at this time of night wouldn't necessarily be Jon.

The pounding started up again and Sam struggled to his feet, yipping softly.

She swung out of bed, looked around for a robe to cover the T-shirt that almost reached her knees, and didn't find one. She gave up the search. Sam accompanied her, although his sleep-droopy eyes told her the dog wouldn't be much help in an emergency.

"I was ready to knock the door down," Jon said when she let him in.

"Sam would have torn you limb from limb," she said, as the dog collapsed in a heap at Jon's feet and rolled onto his back for a tummy rub. "He's trained to kill."

Neither of them cracked a smile.

"I don't want you to go with me." Jon's words sounded like a challenge.

Her hopes crumbled. "You don't?"

"No. I want to stay here. With you."

"But Jon, the job...your dream..." She was determined not to allow tears to form in her eyes.

Jon stepped over Sam and took Amy in his arms.

"You're my dream," he whispered. "Come be my family, Amy Hardaway. Marry me."

The plea startled her, drying the tears that threatened to spill from her eyes. "Oh, Jon, no. I can't interfere with—"

He tipped her chin up and covered her lips with his, halting her anxious words. His lips coaxed hers to soft surrender. Her worries began to retreat. Jon's arms felt like a safe haven from the hurt and insecurity her world held in such abundance these days.

She wanted to say yes, more than anything.

"Say yes," he murmured against her lips.

"But—"

"I told them I'd take the job under one condition."

She looked at him with a question in her eyes.

"That they locate their headquarters in Hurricane Beach."

"Oh, Jon, they couldn't—"

"Yes, they could. In fact, they were astounded by the brilliance of my suggestion when I gave them comparisons of building headquarters in South Florida versus here."

"But your family, Jon. You wanted to get away from your family."

"I don't need to run away from home anymore. Maybe I finally grew up. It happens, you know. Besides, Kieran needs you. The kid has offered to do community service to pay back the money Hardball escaped with. And the people of Hurricane Beach seem ready to give her a second chance."

Amy's eyes grew wide. "I'm glad. She's been through a lot. But Jon, I'm not up to being a stepmother. I—"

"Amy Hardaway isn't up to taking on a little problem like a teenager who's about to flunk out of school?"

"Well…"

Sam woofed. Jon looked down and said, "Okay, mutt, so you were right about what would push her buttons. I'll listen next time."

Amy chuckled. "You've been plotting against me with my dog?"

"Whatever works."

The tears began to well up again, because in his teasing response she heard a truth that she believed in. Whatever they needed to do to make this work, they would do it. Because they were right together.

"I love you, Amy."

"And I love you, Jon."

"Enough to take a chance?"

Amy thought of all the shaky relationships in her life. With Lisa, with Megan, with her parents. Then she thought of how solid things felt with Jon. She thought of feeling that solid ground beneath her feet every day, from now on, no matter what else happened.

"It's going to be stormy," she said, wanting just a little more encouragement.

"Life's always stormy," he said. "There's nowhere to hide from that."

"There's one place," she said, after studying his always inscrutable coffee-brown eyes and realizing she could see what was in them, after all. They told her he had needs and wants and doubts and fears, just as she did. But they also told her Jon loved her, so together they could meet needs and satisfy wants and overcome doubts and fears.

"What place is that?"

In response, she wrapped her arms around him and waited for his to settle around her. Together, they found the place they were looking for.

\* \* \* \* \*

*Be sure to read Lisa Hardaway's story in LISA by Ellen James, the next title in the compelling SISTERS trilogy.*
*Available in May 1997,*
*wherever Harlequin books are sold.*

# HARLEQUIN SUPERROMANCE®

A trilogy by three of your favorite authors.

### Peg Sutherland
### Ellen James
### Marisa Carroll

A golden wedding *usually* means a family celebration.

But the Hardaway sisters drifted apart years ago. And each has her own reason for wanting no part of a family reunion. As plans for the party proceed, tensions mount, and it begins to look as if their parents' marriage might fall apart before the big event. Can the daughters put aside old hurts and betrayals...for the sake of the family?

Follow the fortunes of AMY, LISA and MEGAN in these three dramatic love stories.

April 1997—AMY  by Peg Sutherland
May 1997—LISA  by Ellen James
June 1997—MEGAN  by Marisa Carroll

Available wherever Harlequin books are sold.

Look us up on-line at: http://www.romance.net          SIS

**HARLEQUIN®** *Temptation.*

**and**

**HARLEQUIN®**

# I N T R I G U E®

## *Double Dare* ya!

Identical twin authors Patricia Ryan and
Pamela Burford bring you a dynamic duo of
books that just happen to feature identical twins.

Meet Emma, the shy one, and her diva double,
Zara. Be prepared for twice the pleasure and
twice the excitement as they give two
unsuspecting men trouble times two!

In April, the scorching **Harlequin Temptation** novel
#631 **Twice the Spice** by Patricia Ryan

In May, the suspenseful **Harlequin Intrigue** novel
#420 **Twice Burned** by Pamela Burford

### *Pick up both—if you dare....*

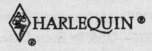

**HARLEQUIN®**

Look us up on-line at: http://www.romance.net          TWIN

*It's hot...and it's out of control!*

Beginning this spring, Temptation turns up the *heat*. Look for these bold, provocative, *ultra*sexy books!

**#629 OUTRAGEOUS**
by Lori Foster (April 1997)

**#639 RESTLESS NIGHTS**
by Tiffany White (June 1997)

**#649 NIGHT RHYTHMS**
by Elda Minger (Sept. 1997)

**BLAZE: Red-hot reads—only from**

Look us up on-line at: http://www.romance.net          BLAZE

# HARLEQUIN SUPERROMANCE®

## WOMEN WHO Dare

## NOBODY DOES IT BETTER
### (#741, May 1997)
### by Jan Freed

It took brains, independence and nerves of steel for Hope Manning to get where she is today, CEO of her own company. And *nobody does it better.*

Jared Austin teaches others to find the peace he himself discovered on a wilderness survival course. And *nobody does it better.*

Blackmailed into "chilling out," Hope reluctantly joins one of Jared's west Texas wilderness expeditions. And it's war between the sexes from the start! Then a sniper appears, gunning for Hope. To survive, she and Jared have to put aside their differences and work as a team....

*And* nobody *does it better!*

Look us up on-line at: http://www.romance.net     WWD-597

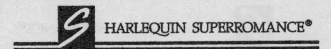

# HARLEQUIN SUPERROMANCE®

## THE OTHER AMANDA
### by
### Lynn Leslie

#### Superromance #735

**Who Is She?**

Amanda Braithwaite has been found nearly beaten to death in a park. At least, everyone *calls* her Amanda—her aunt, her uncle, her grandmother, her doctors. But Amanda remembers nothing, remembers no one. Except Dr. Jonathan Taylor. He saved her life, and he knows more about her than he'll reveal....

Does she really *want* to know the truth, or is the past too painful to remember?

Look for *The Other Amanda* in April
wherever Harlequin books are sold.

Look us up on-line at: http://www.romance.net

LOVE-497

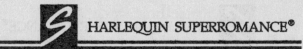

## HARLEQUIN SUPERROMANCE®

## THE MIRACLE BABY
by
## Janice Kay Johnson

If having a baby with a stranger is what it'll take to save her eleven-year-old daughter's life...Beth McCabe is willing to have one.

*Is the stranger?*

Nate McCabe hasn't seen or spoken to his identical twin brother, Rob, for fifteen years. Now Rob is dead and Nate learns that Rob's widow, Beth, and her young daughter, Mandy, need him—but only because he's Rob's twin. Only because they need a miracle.

Mandy will die without a bone marrow transplant. When Nate's tissue fails to match, Beth persuades him to step into his brother's shoes and father a baby—Beth's baby, a child who has a one-in-four chance of saving Mandy's life.

Watch for *The Miracle Baby* by Janice Kay Johnson.

Available in April 1997,
wherever Harlequin books are sold.

Look us up on-line at: http://www.romance.net          9ML-497

Bestselling Author

# MARGOT DALTON

explores every parent's worst fear...the
disappearance of a child.

# First Impression

Three-year-old Michael Panesivic has vanished.

A witness steps forward—and his story is chilling.
But is he a credible witness or a suspect?

Detective Jackie Kaminsky has three choices:
1) dismiss the man as a nutcase,
2) arrest him as the only suspect,
   or
3) believe him.

But with a little boy's life at stake, she can't afford to
make the wrong choice.

Available in April 1997 at your favorite retail outlet.

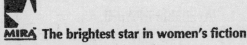 **MIRA** **The brightest star in women's fiction**   MMDFI

Look us up on-line at:http://www.romance.net

# Harlequin® Historical

A clandestine night of passion
An undisclosed identity
A hidden child

**RITA Award nominee**

Miranda Jarrett

presents...

THE SECRETS OF
Catie Hazard

Available in April,
wherever Harlequin Historicals are sold.

Look us up on-line at: http://www.romance.net          BIGB97-5